HORSHAM TOWNSHIP LIBRARY
435 BABYLON RD., HORSHAM, PA 19044-1224
3 1224 1018 4164 0

D0853159

The Girl with the Ghost Machine

Also by Lauren DeStefano

A Curious Tale of the In-Between

The Peculiar Night of the Blue Heart

Lauren DeStefano

BLOOMSBURY
NEW YORK LONDON OXFORD NEW DELHI SYDNEY

First published in the United States of America in June 2017
by Bloomsbury Children's Books
www.bloomsbury.com

For information about permission to reproduce selections from this book, write to Permissions, Bloomsbury Children's Books, 1385 Broadway, New York, New York 10018
Bloomsbury books may be purchased for business or promotional use. For information on bulk purchases please contact Macmillan Corporate and Premium Sales Department at specialmarkets@macmillan.com

Library of Congress Cataloging-in-Publication Data
Names: DeStefano, Lauren, author.
Title: The girl with the ghost machine / by Lauren DeStefano.
Description: New York : Bloomsbury Children's Books, 2017.
Summary: Neglected by her father, who spends all of his time building a ghost machine to bring her mother back from the dead, twelve-year-old Emmaline decides that the only way to bring her father back will be to make the ghost machine work, or destroy it forever.
Identifiers: LCCN 2016044512 (print) • LCCN 2017011490 (e-book)
ISBN 978-1-68119-444-8 (hardcover) • ISBN 978-1-68119-445-5 (e-book)
Subjects: | CYAC: Grief—Fiction. | Fathers and daughters—Fiction. | Dead—Fiction. | Ghosts—Fiction. | Inventions—Fiction. | Science fiction. | BISAC: JUVENILE FICTION / Fantasy & Magic. | JUVENILE NONFICTION / Social Issues / Death & Dying. | JUVENILE FICTION / Science Fiction.
Classification: LCC PZ7.D47 Gi 2017 (print) | LCC PZ7.D47 (e-book) | DDC [Fic]—dc23
LC record available at https://lccn.loc.gov/2016044512

Book design by Amanda Bartlett
Typeset by Westchester Publishing Services
Printed and bound in the U.S.A. by Berryville Graphics Inc., Berryville, Virginia
2 4 6 8 10 9 7 5 3 1

For my mom.

Sorry that this book made you sad.

When the rain falls and enters
The earth, when a pearl drops into
The depth of the sea, you can
Dive in the sea and find the
Pearl, you can dig in the earth
And find the water. But no one
Has ever come back from the
Underground Springs.

—Mei Yaochen

The Girl with the Ghost Machine

Emmaline Beaumont was ten and one quarter when her father started building the ghost machine. It was one month after her mother's funeral exactly.

To some, the pursuit of ghosts might have seemed greedy, given all that life had to offer. There was no shortage of living things in the world, to be sure. Even the rabbits that chewed through their vegetable garden, the chipmunks that left holes in the dirt, the Rousseau family across the alley whose records played at all hours and whose children drew pictures in the fog of their breath on every window from Saint Laurent street to the school.

But when Emmaline's mother, Margeaux Beaumont, died, it seemed as though everything else had died with her. Emmaline and her father could no longer see the colors in the trees. They could no longer hear the melody in music. The vegetable garden became overrun by weeds, and the carrots and the tomatoes turned gray and shriveled.

Emmaline herself hardly spoke in the first month after her mother's death, sustaining herself on the chocolate cherries her mother kept hidden under the sink, salting them with her tears.

Every day since her mother's death, Emmaline wore a single black lace glove on her left hand, closest to her heart.

The curtains were always drawn, and the house was always dark.

This was before Emmaline's father got the idea for the ghost machine.

One day, two months after Emmaline's mother had died, and neither Emmaline nor her father had left the house but to retrieve the mail, Mademoiselle Chaveau, who taught at the school, hammered the iron knocker on the door until at last someone answered.

"Enough of this now, enough," Mademoiselle Chaveau had cried. "You can't have that child living in a morgue. She needs to be in school."

And so Emmaline returned to her lessons, and when she came home in the afternoons, sunlight filled her light honey-colored hair. The smell of autumn burrowed in the fibers of her sweater. She was brimming with jokes and whispers and giggles she had collected all day like stones in her pockets.

And it was then, just as life had begun to make sense to Emmaline again, that the ghost machine came about. She returned from school one afternoon to find her father in the basement, crouched over scraps of metal and foraging through jars of bolts and rusted nails.

Soon thereafter, Julien became the subject of whispers and rumors on Saint Laurent street. He shuttered himself in the basement for hours each day, and all anyone heard was the clang and clatter of machinery and the occasional muttered curse.

Some believed the loss of his wife had driven him mad. Neighbors would knock on the door, bearing covered dishes and freshly baked treats, all hoping to catch a glimpse of whatever he did in that gloomy house. But if he answered the door at all, it was never for more than a fleeting moment, just long enough to mutter a word of thanks.

At ten and one quarter years old, Emmaline was old enough to know that a ghost machine wasn't a very realistic idea. The world was filled with bolts and gears and flickering

light bulbs, and if these things could somehow summon ghosts, it surely would have happened by now.

But still, she had hoped, despite all reason, that it might work. The house was quiet and lonely without her mother to straighten its picture frames and draw its curtains and fill the rooms up with her humming. Now, dishes piled in the sink, and the kitchen table was littered with bills and cards expressing sympathy, and an uncapped jar of honey whose contents had dribbled out onto the week-old newspaper resting beneath it.

And though the idea of summoning ghosts sounded rather odd, Emmaline knew also that there was nothing odd about her father. Rather, he had loved her mother very much. Margeaux Beaumont had left them quite suddenly, after a short and unexpected illness, and there simply hadn't been time to prepare for such tremendous sorrow. When Margeaux died, her coffee cup was still in the sink, soaking in pink

suds that shined and shimmered. Her slippers were neatly placed near the bathtub, and an oval nest of her fine gold hair was still caught in the brush beside the bathroom sink.

And so, when her father began collecting pieces for the machine, Emmaline helped him. She brought him little rusted gears and nails—things she found on the side of the road mostly—and discarded paper clips that were bent out of shape. She collected and rinsed out empty marmalade jars and cans, all the while knowing that these mundane things could not possibly bring her mother back to her. Even so, that small bit of hope was what made her go on foraging for supplies.

One afternoon she pushed an old deflated tire up the steps. Her father was so pleased by this offering that he hugged her until her feet left the ground and he twirled her across the kitchen and kissed the top of her hair.

That was when she asked him, "Papa, what will this machine do?"

His answer was simple. "It will summon ghosts."

"But *how*, Papa?"

"Think of the puddles in the street after it rains," her father said. "Where do they go?"

"I suppose they disappear," Emmaline answered.

He tapped her nose. "They don't disappear. They evaporate. The clouds gather them up, and when it's time, they come back again as rain. Your mother is just like that."

"Mama is in a cloud?" Emmaline asked, skeptical.

"She's not in a cloud, exactly," her father said. "But she's somewhere out there, where things go when it seems like they've disappeared. She can't come back and live with us because her body is gone now, but bodies aren't the most important part of us. The special part, the true part, evaporates when we die. This machine will bring that part back. As to how it will work, that is a small matter to sort out." Her father waved his hand as though swatting away a fly. "It will all make sense once it's done. You'll see."

At first, the machine was strictly off limits. Emmaline would hear her father tinkering and toiling—very rarely shouting, often grumbling—behind the closed door of the basement. Emmaline had never particularly liked the basement. It was dark and damp and full of spiders. But whenever she brought her father pieces for his machine, she found herself trying to peer into the dark stairwell over his shoulder, wanting to catch a glimpse of this thing that had come to consume him. But he always closed the door before she could see.

With time, her father became as inaccessible as the machine. He stopped answering the door when she knocked. He was still in the basement when Emmaline returned from school in the afternoons. At 3:05 precisely, she would leave a sandwich on a plate at the top of the stairs. She would knock on the basement door only once, for she knew her father would know what it meant.

Sometimes her father would retrieve the sandwich promptly. But sometimes—in fact, most times—the sandwich was still there in the evening when Emmaline emerged from her bath and had begun to prepare for bed.

“Good night, Papa,” Emmaline would say on such occasions.

The only response would be the clatter and clamor of tools and gears.

Faced with the quiet of an empty house, Emmaline began to grieve for her father as well. He was still alive, but he was as gone as the dead for as little as she saw of him.

Late one night, kept awake by the thunking and banging in the basement, she climbed out of bed and made her way to the basement, and threw open the door.

Her father didn’t notice at first, lost as he was in his work. He didn’t hear her until she had reached the bottom step.

And just like that, Emmaline had her first look at the thing that had taken up all her father's time. The thing into which he had poured all his hopes. The thing he believed would bring Margeaux back.

Even though the thing did not work—had never worked—Emmaline was rendered speechless by the sight of it. It was a hulking thing, nearly as high as the ceiling. It was a great metal monster, with hundreds of bolts for eyes, and a rectangular mouth, into which Emmaline supposed something was meant to be deposited the way old clothes were deposited into a donation bin.

The basement itself was dark, but the ghost machine created its own light once Emmaline reached the bottom step. A flickering, eerie purple glow that came through all the cracks and corners of the fused metal.

It was unlike anything Emmaline had ever seen. She wouldn't know how to describe such a thing, much less how to describe the way it made her feel betrayed by her own sense of logic. She knew what machines were supposed to look like. She knew what death meant, and that ghosts weren't real. But this machine, frightening and amazing at the same time, made her feel as though anything was possible. It might even be possible for her mother's ghost to emerge from that peculiar glow.

She had expected her father to be angry with her for bursting into the basement, but when he saw the look of wonder on her face, he only smiled.

Chapter 2

It had been two years since the start of the ghost machine's assembly now. Emmaline was twelve and one quarter, and half a foot taller, and the machine still did not work.

Emmaline didn't understand how it would ever work, or why it ate up so much electricity. She kept it a secret, fearing her father would be deemed mad and she would be taken from him.

It had been two years since Emmaline first laid eyes on the ghost machine, and it hadn't been much discussed with her father since.

But it was always there, even if Emmaline rarely was able to go down to the basement and have a good look at it. The ghost machine had become sort of like a stepmother to her, Emmaline thought, the way her father lavished it with affection. The ghost machine took and took her father's love, and offered nothing in return. Even the hope once implied by its presence was gone.

It took two years for Emmaline to work up the nerve to say what she had been thinking for a very long time. She planned it very carefully, turning the words over and over in her head, and then whispering them to her bedroom mirror that morning, until they were smoothed and polished as a stone.

She took a deep breath and then descended the stairs. Mornings were the only opportunity she would have to speak to her father. It was a very short window before he disappeared into the basement, where he would still be until long after she'd gone to bed.

He was at the kitchen table, his elbow resting on a scant three inches of clear space amid the clutter, sipping tea and staring at the newspaper in his lap. The paper was a week old, but the fact that he was reading about the outside world at all was a good sign, Emmaline thought.

"Papa," she said, her voice strong and clear. She straightened the hemline of her jumper. "I have something to tell you."

Her father barely afforded her a glance. "You should have breakfast," he said. "There are some bananas on the counter."

"They've gone bad," Emmaline said. "Papa, it's about the machine. I'd like you to unplug it."

At last, her father looked up from his paper. He set down his tea.

"Unplug it?"

Now that she had her father's attention, Emmaline felt all the words she had planned escaping her. They flew right out of her head and fluttered away.

She stood up straighter.

"It would be for the best," she said. "Mama is—gone—" That word caught in her throat. Even after two years, she would never be used to the idea that her mother wasn't coming home, and it felt wrong to say. She went on, "And she wouldn't want you to spend all your time in the basement trying to bring her back."

"She isn't gone," her father said, his voice soft and gentle, as if he were reading her a bedtime story. "She's somewhere, but she can't find her way back to us. That's all. The machine will help her find a way, like a lighthouse beam."

Emmaline could feel herself shaking, deep down in her bones. Her head felt foggy, the way it always did when she was about to cry.

Don't cry, she told herself. *Remember what you practiced.* But she could no longer remember the words she had practiced. It was far easier to come up with a good argument when she was alone in her bedroom. But here, faced with her father's stubbornness, she remembered all at once why she hadn't brought this matter up at all in the past two years. It didn't matter what she said. He would never listen.

"Mama isn't 'somewhere,'" Emmaline said firmly. "She's in the cemetery, with about a hundred other people, and none of them are going to come back. None of them are ever going to come back, Papa. Everyone in the world knows that's what it means when people die. Everyone except for you."

"Everyone knew that light came from candles," her father said, still in that dulcet tone. "If everyone had accepted that, we would never have light bulbs. We would never have electricity at all. The solution is there, Emmaline. It just takes someone brave enough to find it."

He frowned and reached for her hands, and that's the moment Emmaline realized that she had started to cry. She knew that she had lost, that she would always lose when it came to that machine.

"This isn't like that." Her voice cracked. She backed out of the kitchen and made her way to the door, roughly pulling her coat and satchel down from their hooks.

"Emmaline, please," her father said. "Stay and talk for a minute. I don't want you to go to school upset."

Emmaline pulled the door open. "Why should it start to matter to you now?" she said. She slammed the door behind her.

As she hurried down the sidewalk, she wiped away her tears and then stopped to compose herself. She would catch up with Gully and Oliver DePaul on the way to school, and she preferred not to discuss the ghost machine with her best friends. She would much rather leave that thing in the basement and out of her life.

After two years of losing her father to his own invention, Emmaline was sure that she could never convince him to abandon his project. One of two things must happen. She would have to make the ghost machine work, or she would have to destroy it so terribly that all hope of repairing it would die as her mother had died, and her father would be forced to focus on the living again.

Chapter 3

At night, the November wind moved the trees so that it sounded as though they were breathing.

Emmaline awoke to a branch rapping at her window, and for a sleepy moment she thought her father's machine worked and that her mother's ghost had come to visit.

But then Emmaline saw the branch and was angry with herself for having hoped.

It was late, but Emmaline found herself unable to fall back asleep. The scratching of branches and the howling of wind filled her with an odd sense of worry, and she got out of bed to fix a glass of tea and honey. It was something her mother used to fix for her at night, and even now the bittersweet taste made Emmaline feel safe and warm enough to go back to sleep on nights like these.

Emmaline prepared her tea and sat at the kitchen table to drink it. She had to push aside a stack of books and brush away a cobweb just to have a spot to rest her tea on the table. Once, the kitchen table had been an important place, where she sat in the morning with her parents to eat toast and jam before school, and where she sat again in the evening and they all talked about their day.

Now, the table had become a place to put things that had no proper place. Bills—some opened and some not—plates that attracted lines of ants, chocolate wrappers from the only meals her father sometimes ate for days, books about the psychology of grieving, which Emmaline's aunt liked to send her father by post.

But even though it was cluttered, Emmaline liked to sit at the table and drink her tea. She could still pretend that her mother and father would soon be downstairs to join her.

The house wasn't completely quiet. It never was. Even late at night, the machine continued to eat up the electricity. During the day, it made the lights flicker, but at night it hissed and plinked.

It was especially loud tonight. Emmaline rose from the table and moved toward the basement to investigate. It was rare for her to have a good look at the machine—her father usually shooed her back up the stairs. But he had gone to bed for the night; Emmaline had heard him snoring.

Cradling the teacup in her hands for warmth, Emmaline made her way down the basement steps. It was dark. Her father had removed most of the light bulbs after the ghost machine had shorted out the power circuit enough times.

The engine was always running, and it had a whisper to it, as though it told tales in long-lost languages.

Emmaline realized at once that she hated the machine. She'd once thought that building it would make her father happy, but it had instead consumed him. It caused him to skip meals, to lose sleep, to let the house fall into disrepair. He had even forgotten Emmaline's twelfth birthday, and she hadn't complained because she'd told herself that what he was doing down in this basement was important.

But it wasn't important. It was futile. Her mother was not like the puddles that evaporated. She was not rain, and she wasn't coming back. This machine wasn't going to change that. All it was going to do was continue to steal the only parent she had left.

As Emmaline approached the machine, its

otherworldly glow painted her skin a deep shade of purple. Its incessant humming disturbed the tea in her cup, causing it to ripple.

It wasn't her hatred for the machine that caused her to do what she did next. It was her love for her father.

At the front of the machine there was a rectangular mouth, the source of all the light. Emmaline didn't know what it was for, but it seemed vital, like an exposed heart.

Before she could stop herself, she poured her tea into the rectangular mouth, until the cup was empty. She knew that she might regret this later, but right then her anger clouded her judgment.

The machine growled low. And then it went silent. Emmaline hadn't realized how long it had been since the house was this silent, but now here it was. There was no hum, no thrum, no persistent whirring.

The silence was death. It was her mother's absence. Her true absence, and the promise

that she was dead and buried with no hope of returning.

Emmaline understood immediately what she had done. What she had cost her father. Without his ghost machine to give him hope, he would have to understand that Margeaux Beaumont in all her forms was gone.

The light began to fade, until Emmaline was left standing in blackness. Not even the moonlight could enter through the soot on the tiny basement window.

Her heart was pounding. But she wasn't sorry. She did what needed to be done.

That was her last thought before the machine began to shake, and a burst of light blinded her, and she was thrown off of her feet.

The shrill whine of the teakettle was the next thing Emmaline heard. But that wasn't what truly woke her. It was the voice humming at the top of the basement stairs.

Her face was pressed to the cold, gritty cement floor of the basement, and her head felt stuffed with cotton. It was dark, and at once she remembered what she had done to her father's machine.

"Emmaline," the humming voice called to her. "Emmaline, dearest, don't you want some tea?"

That can't be . . .

"Mama?" Emmaline's head was throbbing and her throat was dry, but these things were secondary. She pushed herself upright.

There was a light coming from the top of the stairs, and a silhouette stood in the doorway. Emmaline's vision was blurred, but it began to clear as she made her way toward the staircase.

It had been so long since Emmaline had seen that familiar shape, that gold hair piled into a bun and pinned with a silver clip. It had been years, and yet it had also been no time at all.

Emmaline looked back into the darkness behind her, where the machine stood dead and still. Had it worked? She looked back to her mother, waiting for her with a cup of tea in either hand.

"Emmaline?"

Her mother didn't look like a ghost. She didn't glow, and her skin wasn't transparent. She looked warm and whole and alive.

Since her father lost himself to the ghost machine, Emmaline had been forced to possess enough logic and practicality for the both of them. But at the sight of her mother, that logic and practicality left her, and she ran until she wrapped her arms around her mother's waist.

Margeaux Beaumont laughed as tea spilled onto the floor from the rattled cups.

"I thought you were gone forever," Emmaline sobbed, squeezing her tighter. "I thought you were never going to come home."

Emmaline felt a gentle kiss on the crown of her hair. Real.

But something wasn't quite right with

Margeaux's voice when she said, "Let's sit and have our tea. We have so much to talk about."

The kitchen table was cluttered as ever, but as Emmaline followed her mother, she could see that a small space had been cleared away so that they could sit and face each other.

Emmaline wanted to ask if her mother was a ghost, but at the same time she didn't want to know. She thought that questioning a thing about this moment would cause it to pop like the soap bubbles she'd tried to keep forever on her fingers when she was little. So she said nothing, and took her tea.

"Your papa hasn't been keeping up with the housework." Margeaux sounded sad. She brushed her fingertips over a dusty book called *Mourning, a Single Parent's Guide*.

"I should help him," Emmaline said.

"You should do no such thing," her mother said. "Your papa should be taking better care of you, not the other way around. I understand full well why you tried to break that machine."

Emmaline started to feel tears filling her eyes again. "I'm sorry, Mama. I never thought that it would work."

Margeaux took a sip from her cup. "Finish your tea; I have to take it with me when I go."

"You have to take the tea?" Emmaline asked, confused. "Take it where?"

Margeaux leaned close, a sad smile on her lips. She brushed the hair from her daughter's face. "It will evaporate."

Emmaline felt the same desperate fear as she'd felt two years ago, when her mother was in bed and burning with a fever no doctor could cure. The feeling of watching something slip away when it was still so loved and needed.

"Can't you stay?" Emmaline asked.

"Do you remember how we'd sit and drink tea during thunderstorms?" Margeaux said. "You were frightened. You thought the thunder would cause the house to collapse."

"But we'd count the silence between the lightning and the thunder, until we knew the storm was moving away," Emmaline said. "I remember." She took a sip of her tea, and it tasted rich and sugary. And then it tasted like nothing at all, and she looked down and saw that her hands were empty.

Emmaline blinked. "Mama?" she said. But the only one in the room was Emmaline, sitting alone at the messy kitchen table piled with neglected bills and dishes.

For a moment, she felt as though her mother were simply in the next room, or upstairs, or even outside, chasing off the raccoon that dug through her garden at night. The word "gone" had meant something different when Emmaline's mother was still alive. A person who was gone would come back.

But then, slowly, the new definition of that word returned to her. The real definition. Margeaux Beaumont was gone again, and still, and always.

Chapter 4

In the morning, Emmaline awoke with no memory of having gone to bed. There was a rough spot on her tongue from where the tea had burned it. She remembered drinking it in haste because she was afraid that it would disappear.

She ran down the stairs and found her father, muttering as he dug through the clutter that had spread from the table to the countertops. "Emmaline, have you seen my wrench? The one with the orange handle. It has to be that one."

Her heart fell to her feet. “No, Papa.”

“I’ve asked you a thousand times not to move the things on the table. They’re important, all of them.”

“I didn’t.” Her voice trailed as she looked to the sink. But there was no trace of the teacups or the kettle.

It hadn’t been a dream. Emmaline was quite sure. Her mother had been here.

But she couldn’t tell her father. Not yet. Not until she knew what exactly had happened after she broke the machine.

She returned to her bedroom and dressed for school, and as she stood in the mirror she saw a scrape on her arm from when she’d been thrown away from the machine.

“It worked,” she whispered to her own reflection.

But what was it her mother had said? Her mother had asked her if she remembered something about thunderstorms, and now Emmaline had forgotten.

She was still trying to remember as she walked to school, but it was as though someone had gone through her memories and colored over bits of them with a black crayon.

As always, Gully and Oliver met up with her at the intersection by the ancient cemetery.

They were twins, and utterly identical, save for the faint white scar under Oliver's left eye. Even their curly black hair fell in the same messy tangle, and their eyes were the color of the sky when it turned dark early in the winter.

They began to walk the remaining three blocks to school, and it took nearly half that time for the twins to realize that Emmaline was not trying to moderate their argument the way she always did.

"Emmy?" Oliver said. He had the softer voice of the two, and a more prominent line in his brow when he was concerned. He petted her shoulder. "What's the matter?"

Emmaline bit her lip. The three of them

talked about everything—except her father's ghost machine. The twins knew how much it pained her, and anyway, Emmaline didn't know what to say. She didn't know how to explain that her father couldn't pick her up from school when she was sick with a fever last June because he hadn't answered the telephone, or that he never visited her mother's grave in the day, only at night when there would be no one to pass on the streets, or that the power in the house was always flickering and the bill was so high that Emmaline hadn't had new shoes in well over a year, because she didn't want to ask him for money and he hadn't noticed their state of disrepair or how tight they had become.

She would rather talk about lighter things, anyway. And the twins always made her laugh. Made her feel like things were normal until she climbed the steps to her home and walked inside.

But all of that was before the machine had worked.

When she didn't answer, even Gully started to look concerned. "What is it?" he asked.

Emmaline stopped walking. They were standing at the end of the cemetery. It ended abruptly with a sharp turn that led into the shopping center. All those gravestones gave way to cafés and the bakery that made the mornings smell like spiced cinnamon and caramel. Death turned into the hope of living things.

Emmaline had never noticed the contrast before, when her mother was still alive.

She looked between the twins. "What if," she began, and paused. "What if my father's machine could work? What would you think?"

"I'd want to see Tidbit again," Oliver said, with the sweetness Emmaline admired about him. Tidbit had been their dog—an enthusiastic old bloodhound with a copper coat and persistent bark.

But Gully spent a great deal of time thinking things through. More so than his brother. He was twelve and three quarters, but his eyes were years older. "Do you want the truth?" he asked, his voice low and serious.

"Yes," Emmaline said. "Of course."

"I wouldn't want to see anyone again. Not if they've died." He looked at his brother. "Tidbit had a good life. A long one. He's happy wherever he is now."

"But who is feeding him?" Oliver said. "Who knows that he needs someone to throw the orange ball around the yard after dinner so that he'll be tired? Whose bed is he sleeping on?"

"Don't be dumb. None of that matters when you die."

"Someone has to take care of him," Oliver countered. "Just because he's dead doesn't mean he won't want somebody to play with."

They began to argue, and Emmaline looked to the graves. Gully and Oliver had never lost their mother. They knew where she was, and that she would be there when they came home, and that the kitchen would smell of the pie-scented candles she burned on the shelf above the stove. This was something that Emmaline couldn't explain, and losing someone they loved was not something she wanted them to understand, besides.

"Emmaline." Gully's voice brought her out of her thoughts. She turned and found herself looking right into his eyes. "Did something happen with the machine?"

Oliver was looking at her just as intensely. "Did it work?"

"I—I think it did," Emmaline said. "Actually, I know it worked." She looked around to be sure they were alone on the sidewalk. "I was so fed up with the machine that I did something horrible and tried to break it. But instead, I somehow made it work. It sparked, and threw me across the room." She held up her arm, showing them the scrape as evidence. "And the next thing I knew, my mother was upstairs, calling for me."

Gully's concern grew. He touched her forehead, checking for a fever. He didn't find one, which only seemed to concern him more. “I think you hit your head when the machine threw you. Have you noticed anything else strange? Any ringing in your ears?”

Emmaline sighed, frustrated. “It was real. I poured my tea into the machine and my mother came back.” It sounded more absurd the more she tried to explain it, and her voice cracked. “She was just as I remembered her.”

“Oh, Emmy.” Oliver frowned sympathetically. “I believe you.”

Gully looked conflicted. “The bell is going to ring soon,” he said. “We should go.”

Gully knew that they would make it to school just in time for the bell if they started walking now. It took one and a half seconds to walk across one square in the sidewalk, and three seconds to cross the driveways in front of the nine storefronts, and seven to cross the street—or ten if Oliver dragged his feet, which he often did. From the cemetery, this added up to two minutes and fourteen seconds.

Gully was always keeping track of things. He only faltered when it came to Emmaline, who changed from one day to the next. Who smiled when she was sad. Who was patient when she had every right to be angry. Who was thoughtful and often secretive.

He couldn't figure her out, but still he liked to try.

And by noon, Gully knew that something had surely changed in Emmaline. She had been very quiet and still all morning in class. Pencil in hand, she had only drawn senseless lines and shapes on her notepaper, as though she was trying to conjure up a thought that wouldn't surface. She didn't even raise her hand to answer the geography questions, even though geography was her favorite subject and she always studied ahead of the required work.

When it was time for lunch, he watched as Emmaline tore at the skin of an orange, not seeming to care whether or not she could effectively peel it. They sat in the school yard, on a low stone wall that bordered the playground.

"Why did you pour tea into the machine?" Gully asked.

Emmaline raised her head as though waking from a trance. "What? Oh. Because I wanted to break it, like I said."

"Yes, but why tea?" Gully pressed. "Why not regular water, or why didn't you try to hit it with something?"

Emmaline thought about this. "Because," she began, with some difficulty as she grappled to remember, "I had made myself a cup of tea, and something about tea made me think of my mother—although now I'm not sure if that's right. My memory is fuzzy."

"Your mother used to make you tea," Oliver chimed in. "When you were scared of the thunder. That's what you told me." Though Emmaline did not discuss her father's machine, she did often talk about her mother.

"Did I?" Emmaline said. "I can't remember. That's another thing. It feels like pieces of my memories are missing, too."

Emmaline struggled to find a memory of her mother making tea for her during a thunderstorm—even one. Now that Oliver had introduced the idea to her, she knew that the memories were there, and she could sense them, like she was trying to remember the melody of a song heard once and long ago.

"Think hard," Gully said. "What's something you remember about her?"

Immediately, Emmaline recalled a time several years earlier when Monsieur and Madame DePaul had to travel overseas. Gully and Oliver spent a weekend at her house. They gathered all the pillows in the house and made a giant cloud on the living room floor with them, jumping and laughing and stuffing their faces with chocolates and warm milk, until they fell asleep.

Vaguely, Emmaline could recall the storm on the first night, the way that rain poured out of the sky and the windows shook from the force of it. She remembered thunder, and then the warm smell of—something. What was it? Something that had allayed her fears and lured her to the kitchen, the twins at either side of her, all three of them huddled in the same quilt.

But this was where the memory turned black, as though it had been painted over.

She blinked, and Gully and Oliver were both watching her intently.

They were the only friends who had ever really known her mother, and now, the only ones who ever would. And that alone made them all the more special to her.

"I can't remember," she said. "I remember thunderstorms, but not my mother making me a cup of tea. It sounds like something she would have done, but—"

Sadness came over her just then. She had already lost her mother once, and now she felt that she was losing her again. "It's like someone broke into my house while I was sleeping and took some of her pictures off the wall," she said.

Oliver patted her hand, and she couldn't help smiling at him.

Gully stared into the distance, his jaw pushed forward the way it always was when he was thinking hard. "What has your father used to fuel the machine?"

"Electricity," Emmaline said. "And lots of it." She was studying Gully closely. She could see that he was forming some kind of revelation.

"Maybe the machine needs more than electricity," Gully said. "You can use electricity to power a toaster, but you still won't have toast unless you give it bread."

Emmaline was beginning to understand. "You think the tea specifically had something to do with it?"

"Not the tea, but the memory attached to it," Gully said. "Maybe if you feed the machine a memory, that's what makes it work. And now the memory is gone."

"We'd have to experiment," Oliver said, his eyes lighting up. "You have lots of things that remind you of your mother." He nodded to the gold chain that hung from Emmaline's neck, which held an old skeleton key that Emmaline's mother had saved when her childhood home was demolished to build a hotel in the city. "If you fed the machine more things, maybe you'd be able to see your mother again."

Emmaline closed her fist protectively around the key. Tea was one thing, but she couldn't bear to part with any of the treasures her mother had given her.

"Don't get too excited," Gully told his brother. "It's just a theory."

"What else could it possibly be?" Oliver said.

"It could all have been a dream," Gully

reasoned. "Dreams can feel very real, even after you wake up sometimes."

Emmaline was sure that it hadn't been a dream, but she didn't try to argue. Gully was the most logical person she knew. She didn't expect that he would believe something so strange without seeing it for himself.

Still, he continued to think aloud. "It would explain why you don't remember drinking tea with her when you were scared of the thunder," he said. "Putting a memory into the machine is like spending a penny at the arcade. It's gone now."

Emmaline's brows knotted in worry as she considered this. *Gone.* She'd had a moment with her mother, and that short time had been enough to undo two years of grief and longing. But it was gone now, and it had taken a memory with it. Memories, at least, were supposed to be hers to keep. That was how it worked. They lived even when the person in them didn't.

"Have you told your father?" Gully asked.

"No." She forced herself to eat a slice of her orange, considering. After her mother died, Emmaline had learned the importance of meals even when she didn't feel hungry. She knew that this small bit of order would keep her firmly in the world of the living, and she would not drown so readily in sadness. "I don't know if it will even work again. What if I really have broken the machine forever, and he missed out because of me? I couldn't bear to tell him that."

"We can help." Oliver smiled, reassuring her.

They huddled together, and they made their plan. At midnight, after her father had at last gone to bed, they would sneak out of their beds and meet her at her house. They would bring something that held a memory, and she would show it to the machine.

Chapter 5

It was with much debate that Gully and Oliver set about finding a memory to feed to the machine. They finally agreed on a blue plastic plant that had occupied the tank of their long-since-departed goldfish, Maggie. They didn't miss the goldfish nearly as much as Tidbit, and it would be easier to bear, Gully had said.

Emmaline lived in a tall, slender house made of brick, with flower boxes in the windows. They were empty now, save for some dirt and dead vines. The house sat at the heart of a quiet, if overcrowded, street, with narrow alleyways between homes. Gully and Oliver were still arguing about not summoning Tidbit's ghost when they stepped beneath the green overhang at Emmaline's front door.

She had been waiting at the window, and she let them in.

The twins were startled by how chilly and dark the house was, but they didn't remark on it. They knew that Emmaline's father had become stingy about things like electricity and heat since he'd started his machine.

"What did you bring?" Emmaline whispered.

"Fish plant," Oliver replied unhappily.

"I didn't know you had a fish."

"It didn't live for very long," Oliver said. "But maybe it'll be nice to see again."

Emmaline opened the basement door, revealing the purple glow of the machine. "After you," she said.

Gully went first, mystified by the throbbing hum of the machine. He had heard it faintly before, but the door to the basement had always been closed. Now at last he was able to see the thing that had intrigued him for some time.

Swathed in its own glow, the machine was a pile of gears and scrap metal, with a gaping mouth that, combined with two bolts, made it look like an expression of astonishment.

Oliver followed a step behind his brother, his eyes bright with excitement.

Emmaline closed the door behind them, apprehensive.

"Be careful," she said. "When I poured my tea into the machine last night, it threw me back."

Gully took the blue plastic plant from Oliver's hand. He wasn't any bigger or stronger than his brother, but sometimes he seemed to think that he was. "Stand back. I'll do it."

"Wait," Oliver said. "When Maggie comes back, won't she need water?"

“Maggie is dead,” Gully said. “She doesn’t need anything.”

Still, Oliver looked worried. Emmaline held his hand to reassure him, and together they moved out of the way.

“Careful, Gully,” Emmaline said. He was smiling, though, in that studious way he took on whenever he was faced with the potential to learn something new.

He dropped the blue plant into the mouth of the machine, and in that same second, Emmaline grabbed him by the arm and pulled him to safety.

But the machine didn’t spark. It didn’t burst with blinding light or knock them from where they stood.

It was quiet, save for the machine’s persistent hum. Gully’s expectant expression turned thoughtful, then disappointed.

Guilt knotted in Emmaline’s stomach. She *had* broken it. And not only would there never

be another ghost, she would never see her mother again.

And then the machine began to rattle. Oliver twisted his fist around her sleeve and gasped. A moment later, Emmaline saw it: a bright orange goldfish, swimming in the air as though it were water. It sailed across Gully's astonished eyes and swirled around Oliver's head. He giggled as the fin flicked his nose.

Gully held up a finger, and cautiously, thoughtfully, stroked the fish's back. "It's real." He blinked.

"Of course it's real." Oliver laughed.

Maggie, the ghost, spiraled through the air a few more times and then disappeared as though she had never even been there.

Gully was the first to move. He looked behind the machine, to the tangle of wires that led into the wall. He inspected the gears, ran his hand along the smooth metal. He peeked inside the mouth of the machine, squinting at the brightness of it. "The plant we fed it is gone," he said.

"Search your memories," Emmaline said. "Does anything feel like it's unclear?"

Gully looked at her. "I can't remember when we got her."

"Me either," Oliver said. The blue in his dark eyes was shining.

Gully went back to inspecting the machine, and Emmaline peeked over his shoulder. "Don't touch anything," she said.

"Most of these wires seem to be feeding the light bulbs," Gully said. "Why purple bulbs?"

"It was my mother's favorite," Emmaline offered. "If that means anything."

"And the engine is definitely electric." Gully was talking more to himself than to anyone. He slipped his hand in the narrow slot between the machine and the wall. "Plenty of fans are keeping it from overheating, and that's what's draining most of the electricity. The bulbs wouldn't be using too much."

The machine shuddered and clanked, prompting Gully and Emmaline to look at it.

No. The machine hadn't made the noise. It was the sound of something falling *into* the machine.

Oliver stepped back, looking sheepish. He put his hands behind his back.

"What did you do?" Gully demanded.

A dog barked in answer. Emmaline followed Gully's gaze just in time to watch the copper bloodhound leap up and put his paws on Oliver's shoulders and lick his cheeks. Oliver squinted and began to laugh, a loud, uninhibited, happy sound. He wrapped his arms around his dog. "It worked! It's Tidbit!"

"Oliver, how could you?" Gully rasped. But he reached forward to scratch his old dog's ears.

"I put one of his chew toys in the machine. I knew you'd want to see him again, no matter what you said," Oliver told him.

During the last year of his life, Tidbit had been listless and slow, but now that he was a ghost, he was energetic as a puppy. The twins knelt on the ground as Tidbit whimpered his excitement and lapped at their faces.

Emmaline stood at a distance to let the twins have a proper reunion, but she couldn't resist reaching out just once to pet the dog's head, to feel his silky coat.

She was so caught up in how real he was, how much like a living dog the way he panted and whimpered and slobbered, that she almost didn't hear the noise at the top of the stairs.

The door creaked open, and she froze. Dread filled her even before she dared to raise her eyes.

Her father stood at the top of the stairs, and he was staring at Tidbit. He saw him wag his tail and then disappear, leaving Oliver clinging to the air.

"Papa." Emmaline's voice felt far away, drowning in the hum of the machine.

The twins hurried to their feet. Oliver fidgeted, and Gully nudged his shoulder to still him.

For the longest time, Emmaline's father didn't move. He didn't move, and no one spoke.

The dog must have woken him, Emmaline thought. She should have told Gully and Oliver to be quieter. Her father did not sleep very deeply, not since he'd begun making the machine. It was as though the machine had syncopated itself to his heart somehow. This was one of the many things Emmaline resented about the machine, and for a bitter moment, standing there, she wished she really had broken it. She did miss her father so.

"Monsieur Beaumont," Gully began, his tone steady. He always found a way to be steady. "I apologize. I know it's late—"

"Yes," Julien Beaumont interrupted him. His own voice was dazed. His eyes were fixed on the humming machine. "It is quite late. Your parents will be worried if they wake and find you gone. Go on home, boys."

They didn't need to be told twice. Side by side they climbed the steps. Oliver looked over his shoulder to give Emmaline a worried glance. He was biting his lip. Gully tugged him along.

Seconds later, they were gone. Emmaline heard the front door open and close, and then she was alone, standing beside the machine.

"It worked," her father breathed. He didn't sound angry, or happy, or frightened. Emmaline didn't know what to make of him just then. It had been two years since her mother had died, and in that time, there were days when her father almost looked as he once had when her mother's laughter filled the house. And there were days when Emmaline didn't recognize him at all. Did not know what was happening behind his warm eyes.

He thundered down the steps, and he ran once he reached the bottom. Emmaline thought he was running for the machine, but to her surprise he grabbed her and swept her up and spun her around.

It had been so long—so long—since he had done this, but she erupted with a laugh the way she always had before. The moment lasted for a small forever.

After he set her back on her feet, he took her cheeks in his hands. "How? What did you do?"

They sat on the cold basement floor, and Emmaline told him all about the tea and her mother's ghost, and Gully's theory that the machine was using memories as fuel. She told him that her own memory of supposedly having tea with her mother during thunderstorms, as Oliver had said, was scratched out. Missing.

Her father looked to the machine, its purple glow sharpening the edges of his face. He had gotten so much thinner, Emmaline realized.

"Papa," she said. "Once you feed a memory to the machine, it's gone forever. Eventually you'll just run out."

"It's designed to work on memories," he said. "But I had it all wrong. I was writing them down and throwing the paper into the machine. All this time, I should have been using objects associated with the memory."

"But then you can't get it back ever again." For the second time that day, Emmaline clutched the skeleton key hanging from her neck. "It's a high price, Papa."

"This is progress," he said, not seeming to have heard her. "I should dismantle the machine to see if the objects are still inside. Then they can be reused, perhaps. But no—doing that may break it. It's quite a fickle thing." He caught himself rambling and blinked at Emmaline. "All of this can be dealt with in the morning. You have school tomorrow."

Emmaline knew she was being dismissed. She fretted. Tomorrow was in fact Saturday, but she didn't point it out. "Are you coming upstairs, too, Papa?"

He reached forward and tousled her hair. Such a small gesture, but Emmaline clung to it. "In a bit," he said. "I have some things to do. Go on and sleep. It's very late."

Emmaline hid her concern and did as she was told.

As she lay in bed, she waited for the sound of her father's footsteps coming up the stairs, the creak of his door as he went to bed. But the sounds never came, and eventually, Emmaline drifted to sleep.

A soft kiss on her cheek woke her. A cool, soft hand stroking her forehead.

"Mama?" she whispered.

"Yes?"

"Where did you go when you died?"

Her mother's soft laugh made the room go warm. "That's not for you to know. Not for a very, very long time."

"Do you miss us while you're there? Do you wish you could come back home for real?" Emmaline's voice was fading. She could not seem to stay awake.

Her question went unanswered.

She opened her eyes, and no one was there.

Emmaline awoke to the sizzle of bacon on the skillet. The smell of fresh pressed oranges. The static voices in the kitchen radio. And singing. Her father was singing.

In the years since her mother's death, Emmaline had found ways to be happy again. Had found things for her heart to enjoy. But this—this sort of happiness was brighter than all of that. Still wearing her nightgown and tangled sleepy hair, she pushed her feet into her slippers and raced down the stairs.

"Good morning," her father sang to the tune of his song. He stood in a patch of morning sun, skillet in hand, smiling his brightest smile. "I thought you might be hungry. Why don't you set the table?"

The table.

For once, the table was free of clutter. There were no traces of the stacks of paper or the rusted tools that had begun to devour it.

Emmaline stood on tiptoe to retrieve the

plates from the cabinet. She set them before two of the kitchen chairs and aligned the forks and butter knives neatly beside them.

She sat and waited for her father to bring the food to the table before she spoke. She found it difficult to meet his eyes.

"What did you throw into the machine?" she asked softly.

"It doesn't matter," her father said. "Some little thing."

Emmaline scooped some eggs onto her plate and skewered slabs of bacon with her fork. "Oh."

"Emmaline, I want to be sure you understand how special this machine is. You shouldn't have come to the twins before you came to me. If it were to get into the wrong hands, something bad might happen."

"I'm sorry, Papa," she said. A cloud shifted in the autumn sky, darkening the room for a moment. "But they won't tell anyone." She was certain about that. Oliver and Gully kept all her secrets, but she didn't say this.

"I know how special they are to you," her father said. "You've known each other since you were babies. But they must keep this secret, and you can tell no one else, do you understand?"

"Yes," Emmaline said, penitent. "I understand."

She couldn't help staring at her father as he sat in his old usual spot and filled his plate. There was softness in his eyes again. He wasn't consumed by frustration and wild ideas. He wasn't glancing anxiously at the basement door, waiting to leave her and get back to work.

Still, Emmaline knew there was something he wasn't telling her. He had summoned her mother's ghost. She knew it. She sensed it, the way she had sensed the kiss on her cheek during the night. She didn't know what they had talked about, or what he had given up for her brief return. She didn't know what more he was planning.

But when he spoke, all he said was, "There

isn't too much food in the house, is there? I think I've cooked all of it."

There was never much food in the house, in fact, but Emmaline decided not to point this out.

"How would you like to go shopping with me?" he asked.

Emmaline couldn't help the smile that spread from her mouth to her eyes. "Really? You and me?"

He nodded. "You and me."

When they left the house, Emmaline felt certain that there were eyes peeking out at them through the cracks of the curtains. Monsieur Beaumont, outside in full daylight! Dressed in something clean and pressed, even. He held Emmaline's hand, the way he had when her mother had been alive, when he was the happiest anyone could ever be.

He remarked how bright and white the clouds were, like clean linen against the cold blue autumn sky.

The Copper Square Market was a sprawling place. Flowers were for sale just inside the doors—a bright ribbon of blossoms that grew bold and vibrant. Emmaline stopped to smell them, and her father let her select one for them to buy. It was pink and white, and it made Emmaline think of how their garden had once looked in the summer.

They walked amid carts of fruit, vegetables crisp and damp, and they talked, actually talked about something other than ghosts. He asked her about school. He listened when she told him. They bought more eggs, and flour and sugar, and decided to bake a cake for lunch, with mint green frosting and cocoa shavings.

The house was filled with words, and laughter, and life. For the first time in two years, Emmaline could scarcely hear the hum of the ghost machine in the basement.

Chapter 6

In the summer, the lake behind Gully and Oliver's house was great for swimming. There was a cliff pressed up against it, slicing into the perfect, smooth blue, like a chip in a mirror. There was a giant tree that grew at the cliff's edge, from which the twins' father had secured a swing made from rope and an old truck tire.

Emmaline, Gully, and Oliver were once so small that all three of them could sit in the tire at once, and take turns dropping into the lake one at a time. Emmaline liked to go last. She liked to wait until the twins swam away and the water was perfect again, and she could cut straight through it and find herself in a jet stream of bubbles. It felt like flying across the universe, past all the stars, into infinite nothingness.

Now, though, they were all bigger, and they could only fit in the tire one at a time.

It was November, and too cold to swim, but Emmaline sat at the edge of the cliff, considering it. She wanted to feel like she was being shot out into nothingness. For just a few seconds.

Gully sat beside her, his chin on his raised knee. He was watching Oliver, who sat in the tire, propelling himself off the edge of the cliff so that the rope twisted and twisted, causing him to spin.

Though Gully's eyes followed Oliver, they also appeared to be staring straight through him.

"Are you thinking about Tidbit?" Emmaline asked, so softly that only he would hear.

"Hmm?" He blinked, raised his head for a moment, and then returned it to his knee. "I guess I was thinking—was that truly a ghost? Or was it a projection?"

"When I talked to my mother," Emmaline began, thoughtfully, "she was talking to me about things that were happening now. The messy table, and how distant my father has been. She wasn't a projection."

"But then—" Gully's brows drew together. He looked troubled. "Does that mean ghosts are real?"

"They must be," Emmaline said. "Don't you think?"

"I didn't think so," Gully said, careful not to let Oliver hear him. Oliver, with his hopeful spirit and beaming imagination, would tell Gully he was wrong; unlike his brother, Oliver did not believe in absolutes. "It doesn't make sense. Our brains make us who we are. Our hearts keep us alive. Our nerves. Skin." He held out his hand and studied it. "When we die, it stops. It all stops. What is a ghost, if all the things that make you who you are have stopped working?"

Emmaline smoothed the hem of her wool skirt; it was black and came just past her knees, which were covered by gray leggings. "Maybe there are things we can't understand."

"No," Gully said. "If it exists, there's a way to understand it. There's a reason. There's some pattern."

Emmaline thought of her father's theory about evaporation, but it sounded strange in the face of Gully's stalwart logic.

They fell silent. Gully's troubled expression deepened, and Emmaline inched closer to him, so that their shoulders touched. There had to be something more than just brains and nerves and skin, she thought. Gully himself made her think so. Sometimes, it was as though he was looking right into her soul. He was seeing through whatever the world saw in her. He was seeing who she really was, in a way that no one else ever had or, she suspected, ever could.

But she didn't know how to tell him that.

"Maybe you should have broken the machine," he said. He nodded at Oliver, who had stopped spinning and was staring at the reflection of bright autumn leaves on the water's surface. "All Oliver can talk about is seeing Tidbit again. He talks as though Tidbit is still alive. It's . . ." he trailed, looking for the right word.

"Confusing?" Emmaline suggested.

"Yes. We said good-bye. And now it's like he's back, only he isn't. He's still gone." He looked at her. "Does that make sense?"

There was sadness in his eyes. Emmaline found it hard to look at him, suddenly. "That's how I feel about my mother," she said. "I'll always miss her, and of course I want her back. But she's gone, and I know it. And I wish my father would say good-bye to her, too, it's just—" She ran her tongue along the roof of her mouth, still feeling the faint burnt patch from the hot tea. "I really miss her, and to see her again was wonderful."

"She's still here," Gully said, as though it were a simple truth, like the time or the weather. "The time you did have with her makes you who you are. So she's alive as long as you're alive."

The thought filled Emmaline with warmth. And suddenly she was fighting the urge to cry. She had cried many times since her mother's death, but rarely because something had made her this happy.

She composed herself, and when she felt able to speak, she said, "Hot cocoa?"

"Oliver," Gully said. "It's getting cold out. We're going for hot cocoa." He stood, offering his hand to his brother. Oliver ignored it and kicked the edge of the cliff, gaining the momentum he needed to swing back onto the dirt.

Here is the way it had always been: Gully

was born first, by three minutes and fifteen seconds. As they got older, Gully remained a heartbeat ahead of his brother, holding out his hand to pull him up onto steep embankments when they went hiking, forging ahead into dark rooms at night to be sure it was safe, standing on chairs to reach the top shelf so his brother wouldn't have to.

But now that they were twelve and three quarters, Oliver had begun to resist his brother's protectiveness, kindly but firmly forging his own paths—even if it meant walking down the dark and daunting hallway by himself at night when he wanted to use the bathroom or get a glass of water. He had also begun to ignore Gully when he scolded him for climbing fences in a way that snagged his coat, or getting too enthusiastic with the heaps of sugar he spooned into his tea.

They were the same age, after all, and practically grown up.

In the café, the three of them shared a giant

slab of chocolate cake with raspberry filling to go with their cocoa. They didn't talk about the ghost machine. They didn't talk about death, or those who had died, at all. They talked only about things that mattered to the living. The history test next Wednesday, and when they thought it might snow.

Gully leaned in, and the sudden seriousness in his eyes made Emmaline and Oliver stop giggling about snowmen and lean in, too. "Emmy," Gully whispered. "Isn't that your neighbor? Sitting one table over? Don't look."

Emmaline glanced at the next table.

"I said *don't* look."

"How can I know if I can't look?" she whispered back. "But yes, that's Mademoiselle Allemand."

After she made the confirmation, Emmaline realized how strange this was. Mademoiselle Allemand had the appearance of someone who had lived for a hundred years. Her skin was leathery; her mouth was puckered and thin and always painted up by a bright pink lipstick that glowed like a neon sign. She wore layers of fur—a leopard coat, a mink stole, a fox-fur-trimmed hat—all of which looked cumbersome on her short, brittle frame.

Mademoiselle Allemand was part of a set. For as long as Emmaline had been alive, Mademoiselle Allemand had resided in the tall blue house across the street, with her two spinster sisters. All three of them had hair that had been scrubbed silvery white by all the years they had lived, and tiny gemstone eyes in varying shades of blue.

They rarely left the house. Emmaline frequently saw grocers carrying bags to the front step. Occasionally one of the Sisters Allemand would come outside to retrieve Professor Boots, their orange tabby with white paws, who was a master of escape. But that brief chase around the house was as much sunlight as they got.

"I saw her on the way to the lake," Oliver offered. "She was walking into a shop."

Gully narrowed his eyes ponderingly. "I saw her, too."

"Running errands, maybe," Emmaline said, although she had to admit that was highly unusual.

"I think she's following you," Gully said. They were all still whispering.

Emmaline blinked. "Why would she be doing that?"

"She isn't hurting anyone," Oliver said, and sipped his cocoa. "Is she normally nice, Emmy?"

"I don't really know," Emmaline said. "She's never talked to me. She never talks to anyone but her sisters, and her cat."

"We could go to the park," Oliver suggested. "There aren't any stores that way, and there wouldn't be anything for her to do. If she follows us out there, we'll know about it for sure."

"It's probably nothing," Emmaline said. She wasn't sure if she really believed that, but she wanted Gully to stop worrying. He had been lost in thought since she'd first told him that the ghost machine had worked. She knew that she was to blame. "It's getting late, anyway. I should go home and check on my father."

Her father had been out of the basement when she had last seen him. For once, he had been vacuuming the cobwebs from the stairs, in high spirits. But even so, Emmaline couldn't shake the sense of dread that she might come home and find the door to the basement closed, her father once again under the spell of his creation.

She even, she realized, dreaded coming home to find her mother's ghost, smiling sweetly at her, hair all aglow in the late afternoon sun. She dreaded the price paid in the form of another memory, and the renewed loss when her mother left again.

"We'll walk you," Oliver said, rooting his finger around the bottom of the mug to scoop up the last of the cocoa. Emmaline couldn't help smiling at him. There was always something in the world to be happy about, and Oliver found these little things with ease.

They stepped outside, into an autumn sunset that was almost electric in its bright yellows and pinks. The trees were black against the sky, twitching nervously on the breeze.

As they walked, Gully's eyes darted toward the windows they passed. He was looking for glimpses of Mademoiselle Allemand's reflection, Emmaline realized, in case she was following them. But she was nowhere to be seen.

The twins walked Emmaline up to the front door, and Emmaline threw an arm around both of them, gathering them in a hug good-bye.

"I'll see you Monday on the way to school," she told them.

Emmaline waited until they had turned the corner at the end of the block before she stepped inside her house. "Papa?"

The door to the basement was closed. The machine's ever-present hum went on behind it.

"Papa, I've brought you some carrot cake. It's your favorite."

A sound from the basement caught her attention. It was not the same as the machine's usual noise.

She set the bag containing the cake on the table and knocked on the basement door. "Papa?"

Now that she was standing so close, the sound was all that much louder. She turned the knob.

She was greeted by a swarm of glowing beads that hovered in the air.

"Close the door," her father whispered excitedly, from somewhere in the darkness beyond the glow.

"Papa, what—" One of the glowing beads passed before her eyes, and she realized it was not a bead at all. It had wings. "Fireflies?" she gasped.

"*Ghost* fireflies," her father said. "There must be hundreds of them!"

Emmaline reached the bottom of the staircase and twirled to see all the brilliant little glimmers around her.

It took several minutes for them to fade, until there were only a handful left. They scattered and then disappeared into the air, and beyond where they had been, Emmaline could see her father's wild grin. "Emmaline, look." He reached for her head, where a single firefly had landed at the part of her hair. It shifted and sat perched atop his finger, and he held it up for Emmaline to see.

"I think I may have found a way to keep the ghosts around for longer," he said. "I've tried with crickets and bees, even a garter snake—like we used to see in the garden, you know the ones."

Emmaline's brow furrowed. The firefly still did not fade. "You've been down here since I left?" She had been gone with Gully and Oliver for hours.

Her father didn't seem to hear her. "If I

feed the machine a memory, it will produce a ghost. But then that memory is gone forever. So, what if"—his eyes brightened, outshining the insect in their purpose—"we can feed the machine a memory that goes on forever? One that can't simply be burned up like fuel."

Emmaline resented the hope that she felt just then. She knew better than to wish for things like ghosts. She knew that to see her mother again would only double the pain in her heart when she had to go away.

She also resented that the hope and curiosity won out over her logic. "How?" she asked.

"Insects," her father said. "Insects are always around. Spiders under the stairs and flies getting into the house, crickets chirping in the grass. There are too many of them to count. So we give the machine a memory of insects, and it can't possibly burn up all the memories we have of them."

"I don't understand," Emmaline said.

"Think of all the ants in the grass when we

had picnics with your mother," her father said. "We don't need to lose the memory of the picnic to see her again. We feed the machine the memory of the ants instead. There are hundreds of ants. Thousands. Millions. Enough to keep your mother alive with us forever."

"Not alive," Emmaline said.

"Yes, yes, but it will be the same as alive," her father said.

"No, Papa. It won't."

The firefly faded from his fingertip, as though her words had cast it back to oblivion. "Mama isn't alive. She'll never be alive again. She'll never brush her hair or take a long bubble bath or make rings on the cover of her books when she sets down her tea. She's *dead*, Papa." Her voice broke. She didn't realize that she had begun to cry until she heard the tears.

"Emmaline," her father began. But he didn't finish whatever he was going to say. He hugged her, and she collapsed against his stomach, sobbing so hard that she shook. She tightened her arms around him, remembering now all at once what it felt like to have a living parent. Sometimes she forgot.

Julien Beaumont could endure a great many things, but he couldn't stand to see his daughter cry. And it had been such a long time since she had cried. She hid her sorrow for his sake. She appeared to be happy so that he would be happy, too. Even when she was sad, which, some days, Julien knew she was.

Julien led her up the stairs, and Emmaline clung to his shirt and wiped her eyes on his sleeve as they walked. "Maybe a glass of milk will make you feel better," he said sympathetically.

"I brought you some carrot cake from the café," she sniffed.

They sat at the table, which was still free of its clutter. Only the bag from the café sat on its surface, and Emmaline stared at it through the blur of her tears.

Her father poured her a glass of milk, but

she didn't want it. She wanted to throw it over the wires of the machine, to break it forever. But she also knew that she wouldn't. Even if it did more harm than good, she couldn't bear to ruin any chance of seeing her mother again.

"I wish you'd never started building it," she muttered. "I hate that thing. I *hate* it, Papa."

Her father was quiet for a long time. Emmaline saw the sympathy on his face. She saw her own pain mirrored back in his eyes. When he spoke at last, he said, "Maybe a break from the machine would do us both some good."

Emmaline rubbed her eyes with the collar of her turtleneck. "Really?" she said.

"Really. When I spoke to your mother last night—" He paused. He must have heard how simple and beautiful those words were, too. The idea that he had spoken to his wife as though she were still alive— "When I spoke to her, she scolded me for not taking better care of you." He frowned. "Emmaline, I built that machine for the both of us. We were both so

sad, and I knew that there was nothing I could do to make us both feel better. Your mother was the one who took such good care of us. I just wanted to bring her back."

Emmaline's heart felt warm at his words. "You don't have to bring her back," she said. "Mama isn't here to take care of us, but we can take care of each other."

"Yes." He patted her hand. "We can." He tried to hide his sadness in his smile, but Emmaline saw it. She had long since begun to understand that she wasn't enough to make him forget about the machine. She could open the curtains, and water the flower in the pot on the counter, and tell her father nice things, but it just wasn't enough.

CHAPTER 7

At midnight, Emmaline awoke to the sound of the front door opening and closing amid the chime of the church's clock tower. She knew it was her father, embarking on a moonlit visit to her mother's grave. She climbed out of bed and looked through her window. Her father was the only one on the cobbled streets, carrying a fistful of purple bougainvillea blooms. They grew wild along the back fence—her mother's favorite.

Maybe it would be good for him, Emmaline

thought. Maybe he would come to understand that Margeaux Beaumont was buried under a stone there and she wasn't going to come back. Maybe he would grieve. She didn't expect him to move on all at once, but it would be a start if he would just unplug the machine's many wires from the wall so that the lights in the house would stop flickering.

She climbed back into bed and drifted back to sleep.

A sound awoke her—she didn't know how many minutes later. She returned to consciousness as though swimming in the night air. She had been dreaming about swinging from the tire and into the lake.

The sound returned. Footsteps? No—something much heavier. It sounded like something had bumped against the table, unaware of the table's presence in the darkness.

She didn't call out to her father. Something told her that he wasn't the one who had made the sound.

Next there came the creaking of a door. Her heart began thumping at that. The basement door.

She crept out of bed, and even before she'd made it halfway down the stairs, she could smell the cold night air that had been let into the house and gotten trapped there. Someone had come in.

The basement door was left ajar now, letting out a bit of the machine's purple glow.

The twins? Emmaline thought. No. It couldn't be them. They would never walk in uninvited in the middle of the night. They didn't have to sneak in to see the machine; all they ever had to do was ask, and she would take them to it. They knew that.

Then who?

Her heart was beating in her ears now. Her bare feet felt cold against the floorboards as she moved across the living room.

She pushed the basement door all the way open, cringing at its keening creak. She took the first step and clutched the railing, leaning forward to see who was there.

There was a figure standing hunched over the machine, bathed in its light. The figure was poking at the gears and knobs, as though trying to find the button that would make the machine work.

Emmaline blinked at the figure several times, trying to convince herself that she was dreaming, for this was surely too strange to be real. But seconds passed, and she didn't wake.

"Mademoiselle Allemand?" she said.

The figure at the machine started and turned around to face her. It was undoubtedly Mademoiselle Allemand.

"What are you doing here?" the old woman rasped.

"I live here," Emmaline said. "Remember?"

"But you should be in bed," Mademoiselle Allemand replied. "Children should be asleep at this hour."

"You should be next door," Emmaline said.

She had reached the bottom of the stairs, and she held out a cautious hand. "I can walk you back." Mademoiselle Allemand was old, and old people got confused sometimes, she knew. If she was lucky, that was all this was.

Mademoiselle Allemand muttered something about children being inconsequential and returned to prodding at the machine.

Emmaline knew a great deal about manners. Manners had been very important to her mother. And once to her father, before the machine came about. She knew that it would be rude to pry her neighbor away from the machine. She also knew that if her father returned home and discovered Mademoiselle Allemand in his basement, no good would come of it.

"Please stop that," Emmaline said. "You aren't going to make it work. It's just gears and metal. You're wasting your time."

"You're a fibber," Mademoiselle Allemand said. "I heard that dog barking. Woke me out of a sound sleep, it did. I looked in through the window, and I saw that dog disappear like a ghost."

Emmaline's stomach twisted. There was a strip of cardboard barricading the tiny window, but upon closer inspection, there was a tiny sliver through which someone could spy. Hastily, Emmaline fitted it back in place, but the damage had already been done.

Mademoiselle Allemand hit the side of the machine with her fist. "Granville?" she said. "Gran, are you in there?"

Emmaline lurched forward and grabbed her arm. "Please," she said. "My father will be very angry if his machine is damaged."

"Don't be greedy!" Mademoiselle Allemand cried, and Emmaline thought she heard the threat of tears in the words. "You're only a little girl. You haven't been around for many years. You don't know what it feels like to have lost someone a very long time ago."

At that, Emmaline took a step back, and her voice softened. "Who did you lose?" she asked.

Mademoiselle Allemand looked at her, considering. Some of her silver hair had come loose from its bun, making her appear somewhat wild. Her eyes were made bluer by the machine's glow, and in those eyes Emmaline could see that Mademoiselle Allemand had once been young, like her.

"My older brother," Mademoiselle Allemand finally said, with great hesitation. "He died long before you were born."

"I didn't know you had a brother," Emmaline said.

"Yes," Mademoiselle Allemand replied brusquely. "You don't know a great many things."

Emmaline ignored that. The Sisters Allemand were not known for their kindness. They would shout from their windows for children to

get off their lawn—even though no child with any sense would actually set foot on their lawn, and they no doubt had a closet stuffed with the discuses and stray balls and kites that had landed in their yard.

"Tell me then, since I don't know," Emmaline said. "If you could see your brother again, what is it you would want to say to him?"

Mademoiselle Allemand looked startled by the question, as though she hadn't expected a child to ask her such a thing. And once, it wouldn't have been a question Emmaline would have thought to ask. But two years without a mother had given her time to wonder all sorts of things that children with living parents didn't.

For a moment, Mademoiselle Allemand didn't answer. She looked very fatigued, in the way sadness caused, and Emmaline dragged a chair from the dusty recesses of the basement and brought it to her. It had a short leg and it wobbled, but Mademoiselle Allemand didn't seem to mind that as she sat down. She stared at the gaping mouth of the machine as though it were a window into her thoughts. "Lots of things," she whispered at last. "I would want to tell him lots of things."

Emmaline frowned. "Mademoiselle Allemand," she began. "You must tell me one thing you would want from your brother, if you were to have only one more moment with him. One moment that would cost you something you could never get back."

Mademoiselle Allemand took a deep breath, but she didn't appear to be considering the question. She appeared to already know what it was she wanted to say—it was just a matter of whether she trusted Emmaline enough to say it.

"What is it you want from me, child?" is what she did say. "Money? You would extort the coins from an old woman's piggy bank?"

"No." Emmaline placed her hand on Mademoiselle Allemand's shoulder. Her voice was soft. "If you promise to keep it a secret, I will show you how to use the machine. But only once. And before I do, I'd like you to think about whether this is something you really want."

"Of course I want—"

"Just listen," Emmaline said. "I don't want your money. The price to see your brother again is a memory. You must go home, and find something that reminds you of him, and feed it to the machine. Once you've done this, it's gone forever, and you'll have your brother's ghost for a few moments."

Mademoiselle Allemand stared into the machine. Her eyes grew more and more youthful. Perhaps she was afraid.

"Think about it," Emmaline said again, more pointedly this time. "Come and find me if you still want to do it."

The old woman looked at her, and worse than the sadness on her face was the hope. She had lived such a long life, Emmaline thought, and she had many memories. So many she could dive into them the way Emmaline and the twins dove from their tire swing into the shimmering lake. In that way, she was very rich. But each of those memories was still irreplaceable. Even in an ocean of them, a drop was a lot to spare.

After Mademoiselle Allemand went home, Emmaline lay awake in the dark, listening to the clocks volleying seconds back and forth. She had not thought death had plucked so many people from so many lives. Even Gully and Oliver, the happiest, most wonderful friends she knew, were left conflicted and hurt by the death of small things. Even her neighbors, who chased after their cat and slammed doors and blared brass music in the afternoons, had mourned for someone.

The neighbors whispered that her father had been driven mad by grief. Perhaps grief made everyone a little bit mad. Perhaps her father was only the first one to do something about it.

Chapter 8

On the walk home from school, Oliver stopped to pluck the dandelions that sprouted wild between the cracks in the sidewalk. Gully was growing progressively more impatient with him. He kept steady count of how many seconds it took to walk each square in the sidewalk, and Oliver was slowing them down.

"Why are you doing that?" he finally asked.

"It's getting cold," Oliver replied. "Soon

winter is going to come and kill them. I don't want them to go to waste."

Gully rolled his eyes, but Emmaline smiled.

It had been a week since the twins had used the machine. Emmaline had not told them about Mademoiselle Allemand, who hadn't come around since. It would only cause Gully to worry, and Oliver to take pity on the woman and perhaps even implore Emmaline to help her.

Instead, it was nice to talk about something normal. Something that living people tended to, like flowers.

It was the first day of December, and December certainly made its presence known with roaring gusts of icy wind.

Gully dug his hands into his coat pockets. "Let's go to the café," he said.

Emmaline was grateful for this. She wasn't ready yet to return home. Her father was spending more time out of his basement now. He was keeping the house tidy and asking

Emmaline how her day was. But Emmaline knew he was visiting with her mother's ghost while she was at school. She knew he was still trying to find a way to make the machine work without erasing his memories. And she still wished he would stop, while at the same time hoping he would succeed. The whole ordeal left an uneasy feeling in her stomach, and she'd begun spending more time away.

At the café, they ordered cocoa and picked a table by the window. Oliver hardly touched his drink, though, too busy slitting the flower stems with his thumbnail so that he could string them together. Emmaline and Gully talked about their lessons, and the countries they would choose as the subject for their upcoming essays.

These were things living people cared about, Emmaline thought. And just as she smiled about that, a shadow moved over her. Gully stopped talking midsentence. When Emmaline looked up, she saw the Sisters Allemand standing over her. They matched one another like different figurines in a porcelain set, of varying heights and wearing lipsticks in varying shades of neon pink. The shortest sister was the one who had crept into Emmaline's house several nights before, but now it was the tallest sister who spoke.

"We've come to talk to you about your father's machine." All three sisters looked to Gully, who was studying them warily, and to Oliver, who had limp dandelions dangling from his fingers. "Is there somewhere we can go to talk?"

"Here is fine, if you would lower your voice," Emmaline said, and she couldn't help the angry bite to her words. When Mademoiselle Allemand did not return after their conversation, Emmaline had hoped she'd thought better of her decision to summon her brother's ghost.

The sisters looked among one another, having some kind of conversation with their glances. It was peculiar how well they could reach one another, Emmaline thought. Even Gully and Oliver, who were identical twins, didn't seem as attuned to each other as the Sisters Allemand. Emmaline wondered what it had been like when their brother was alive, and if he'd been the same way. Or if he'd felt like an outsider, the way the Sisters Allemand made everyone in the world feel like an outsider.

After a moment, they pulled three chairs from an adjoining table and joined Emmaline and the twins.

Emmaline shifted uneasily as Gully stared at her, his eyes trying to ask her a question. She had not told him about Mademoiselle Allemand's unusual late-night visit to the ghost machine. Foolishly, Emmaline had hoped she could forget the incident and give the appearance of being a normal girl.

The tallest sister nudged the shortest. The shortest sister reached into the pocket of her very fuzzy leopard print sweater. She extracted something hidden by her closed fist, and then she set her fist on the table. When she opened her fist, Emmaline saw a silver pin, glinting as it caught the afternoon light. It was of a biplane, with a propeller that spun just slightly from the motion of Mademoiselle Allemand's hand.

"This belonged to Granville," the shortest sister said.

"He was a pilot," the medium-height sister added, and Emmaline was stricken by the youthful melody of her voice, each syllable like a song. "Long, long ago."

Emmaline looked among the three of them. "If you feed this to the machine, you can never get it back," she said. "And you'll lose a memory associated with it."

"We have dozens of planes," the tallest sister said. "Plenty of memories."

Emmaline reached out and tentatively touched the plane with her fingertip. It looked freshly polished and well cared for.

"Tell me a little bit about why you'd like to

see your brother's ghost," Emmaline said. "A reason beyond missing him."

Oliver reached across the table for the plane, and the tallest sister smacked his hand away. "Granville never believed in banks," she said. "He made lots of money, and he hid it away for his children. The problem is, he hid it so well, even his widow doesn't know where it is. She has lived in their house for thirty years since his death, afraid to sell it because she's sure it's hidden in there somewhere."

"Didn't you look for it?" Oliver said. "Check under the floorboards?"

"Of course we did, child, don't be dense," the shortest sister said. "But he was a clever one, Gran was. The only way to find it is to ask him ourselves."

"He has a granddaughter he never had the chance to meet," the middle sister said. She didn't smile, but her voice was sweet like a smile, anyway. "She's getting married in a few days. We'd like her to have the money, to start her life."

"We know it's what he'd want," the tallest sister said.

Oliver looked at Emmaline. "That's a good reason, Emmy."

Gully nudged him. "Hush."

Emmaline picked up the plane. It felt warm and smooth in her palm. "All right," she said. "I'll help you, on the condition that you don't tell anyone about it."

"We have no one to tell," the tallest sister said.

"I need your word."

"We promise," the Sisters Allemand said in unison.

"Three a.m.," Emmaline said. She knew for certain her father would be asleep by then.

"Three a.m.," the sisters agreed.

They left together, their arms linked, a sweet perfume trailing the air behind them.

They looked rather like one large creature with three heads, Emmaline thought.

Gully leaned forward, watching as Emmaline tucked the plane into her coat pocket. "You didn't tell me that they'd asked about the machine," he said.

"I told Mademoiselle Allemand to think about it carefully," Emmaline said. "I had hoped she wouldn't be back."

"What will you tell your father?" Oliver said.

"Nothing. He can't know about this." A horrible knot had formed in Emmaline's stomach. She stared at her cocoa with disinterest.

Gully frowned, mirroring her expression. "Oh, Emmaline." He sighed. "This is becoming something too big."

"I know," she said sullenly. "But after this, no more. No one else knows about it."

"Maybe it will cheer them up," Oliver said. "Seeing Tidbit cheered me up. Once was all we needed, wasn't it, Gully?"

"Once was too much," Gully corrected. Oliver ignored him. He got up from his chair and walked to Emmaline, and placed the crown of dandelions on her head.

The petals looked like little stars in her honey-colored hair.

"I think it's the right thing to do," Oliver said, sitting in the chair beside Emmaline.

"And why's that?" she asked him.

"Because when we're very old like the Mademoiselles Allemand, I hope that we can use the machine." Gully opened his mouth to speak, but Oliver spoke quickly before Gully could interrupt him. "Once we're so old we can barely even walk without canes, I want us to use the machine again. I want us to have a long life filled with good-byes, all the while knowing that one day we'll get to say hello again. I think that would be nice."

Emmaline smiled. That did sound nice. But then, Oliver had a way of making her see the good in things. He even made her hate the machine a little less, for a moment.

"We'll come with you tonight," Gully offered. "To make sure they don't do anything strange."

What they were doing was already strange, Emmaline thought.

By the time the clock struck three, Emmaline's father was asleep. Emmaline tiptoed out of bed and went to the front door. Gully and Oliver were already waiting on the front step in their heavy wool coats and their scarves—Oliver's red and Gully's bright green.

"Emmaline," Gully said, whispering as she led them into the house, "you don't have to do this. You don't know much about your neighbors. It feels like a bad idea."

She was looking anxiously through the open doorway. "You heard what they said," she told him. "They just want to ask one question, and

then it'll be over. They won't tell anyone. They don't talk to anyone besides their cat."

"I think it's kind of you," Oliver said. But even his sweetness didn't appease Emmaline's worry. Gully was probably right about this being a bad idea. He was always right.

The Sisters Allemand swept across the street in a soundless flutter of fur coats. They didn't say a word as Emmaline led them into the basement, Gully and Oliver in tow, and closed the door behind them.

Standing before the machine, Emmaline took the silver plane from her pocket and held it out to the sisters.

"How much time will this buy us?" the middle sister asked.

"It depends on the strength of the memory, I think," Emmaline said. When she had poured the tea into the machine, her mother's ghost lasted only as long as it would take her to sit and drink a cup of it. But her father's memories had been stronger. She was certain her mother had stayed with him for a long time, perhaps hours.

The tallest sister took the plane, and after the three of them exchanged a look, she dropped it into the machine.

As it fell, the propeller spun, and Emmaline could swear the plane began to fly into the depths of the purple light, until it was gone.

Nothing happened at first, as usual. "Give it a few seconds," Emmaline said. "And then it'll start to rattle." She began climbing the steps, both to afford the sisters some privacy and to make sure her father hadn't woken.

Oliver sat on the bottom step to watch the reunion, but Gully followed her. "Are you all right?" Gully asked, as they stepped into the living room. "I mean, with all of this."

"I still wish my father would destroy the thing," she admitted.

A male voice coming from the basement made them both turn their heads. They couldn't make out the words being spoken, but Emmaline supposed that was the late Granville Allemand.

"I hope they get what they want out of this," Emmaline said.

Gully frowned at her, but he did not say what he was thinking, which was that she was too kind. It seemed an odd thing to believe: that someone could be too kind. And her kindness was what made him ever want to be her friend to begin with. But being kind meant granting requests like these, and Gully did not like the idea of anyone using Emmaline or getting her into trouble on their account.

Several minutes passed, and then the sisters walked up the stairs. They were sobbing and clinging to one another. They addressed Emmaline with a collective nod and sniffles. The shortest one grabbed Emmaline's hand and gave it a grateful squeeze.

Emmaline couldn't help smiling at that. Perhaps, she thought, the machine could serve a good purpose, after all. If it were to be used sensibly. The Sisters Allemand were happy under all those tears, after all.

Gully followed the Sisters Allemand outside, to help them catch their cat, who had not only escaped again but this time had scrambled up a tree.

Emmaline stood in the doorway and watched the scene unfold, her arms folded against the chill.

Oliver fitted his scarf over Emmaline's shoulders like a blanket to keep her warm. She smiled at him.

"Emmy." Oliver's voice was hushed. "You did a very good thing. You helped them."

"Me?" She blinked. "I haven't done anything."

"Of course you have," Oliver said. "I wished you would have stayed to watch. Monsieur Allemand appeared, and it was as though he wasn't a ghost at all. They hugged him, and everyone was crying, and he asked about his wife and his children. He said he thinks of them all the time where he is."

Emmaline toyed with the fringe of the scarf. She knew what it was like to see the ghost of someone she loved. But what Oliver hadn't seen was what came next. Tonight the Sisters Allemand would return to their quiet house, and turn out the light, and go to bed, and search for the memory of their brother they fed to the machine. They would realize that their minds had been prodded and scratched at, like discarded notes on a scrap of paper.

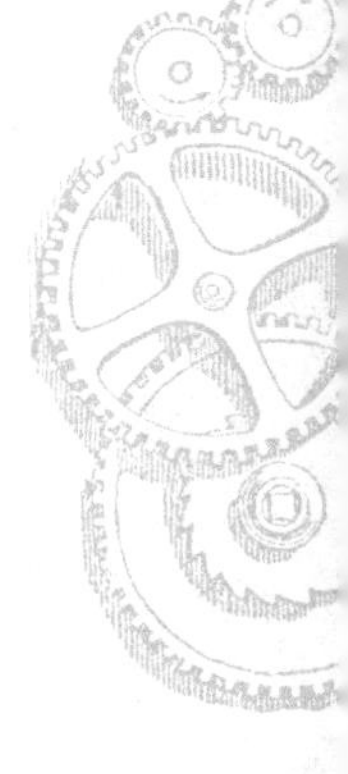

Oliver took her hand and squeezed it. Emmaline wished it could be as simple as Oliver made it seem. She wished all the good that the machine created wasn't undone by the sadness it created, too.

Later, when Emmaline went to bed, she thought about the tiny silver plane flying into the machine, and the tea she'd thrown in anger, and what Oliver had said about her doing a good thing by letting the Sisters Allemand use the machine.

She tossed and turned until the clock struck four.

By four o'clock, Emmaline was no longer thinking about Granville Allemand. She was thinking of her mother. She was trying to see through the black patches in her memory. Something to do with thunderstorms, but what? Something her mother used to say to her—what was it?—a song?—a poem?—maybe just an embrace.

Whatever it had been, it truly was gone forever.

Chapter 9

By morning, Emmaline hadn't gotten much sleep. She descended the staircase and was greeted by the smell of toast and syrup—her favorite.

"I thought you would be hungry," her father said. He was smiling.

Emmaline had a hard time meeting his eyes. She had gone behind his back, and guilt was starting to set in.

She took a bite of her toast, but she wasn't hungry.

"What's the matter?" Her father touched her forehead. "Do you feel sick?"

"No." Her response was too cheerful. "Not at all." She took another bite of toast, summoning more enthusiasm.

Her father prepared a plate for himself and sat down across from her. "How is school?" he asked. "Didn't you say you have an essay due soon?"

Emmaline's mouth rose into a smile she couldn't control. "You remember that?"

"Of course," her father said, and took a sip of his coffee. "You're my daughter."

The guilt Emmaline felt was overwhelmed by warmth. "We have to choose a country to write about," she said. "Gully is going to write about Japan. I haven't decided what I'm going to pick yet, but I'll have to hurry before all the choices I might want are already taken."

"There's some glitter in the scrap drawer from one of your mother's old scrapbooking projects," her father said. "We can use it for your cover page."

"Really?" Emmaline said. "You'll help?"

Her father smiled, but his smile turned sad. "I know that I haven't been around, Emmaline. But I've thought a lot about what you said, and you're right. We need to take care of each other. More importantly, I need to take care of you. You're all I have left."

"You have lots of people who care about you, Papa," Emmaline said. "Aunt Cherelle sends you all those books and letters, and the neighbors ask about you all the time."

"Yes, I suppose," her father said. "But you're the one who matters most."

It was such a beautiful thought. Once, it had gone without saying. When Emmaline was small, she had always felt important. Once. But now, though she feared ruining the sentiment, she had to ask, "Do I matter even more than the machine?"

Her father was wounded by that. Not because she had asked, but because he'd given her such reason to. "Yes," he said. "You matter more than the machine. More than ten of them." He brightened. "In fact, I have an interview this afternoon at the shoe factory."

"You're going to get a job?" Emmaline asked.

"I think it's about time to return to work, wouldn't you say?" he answered. Before his wife's death, he had worked in a patent office, overseeing all manner of strange and peculiar inventions. But then he'd left work to become an inventor in his own right, and after two years of exhausting his resources and forcing both himself and Emmaline to pinch every coin that crossed their paths, money had grown thin.

Before Emmaline could ask her next question, he answered it for her. "I will still work on the ghost machine, Emmy. You have to know I can't give up on it. But it can be more of a weekend project. Or perhaps every other weekend."

It was progress, at least, Emmaline thought.

They ate in silence for a while, each of them considering the conversation and all the changes it would bring. And then Emmaline said, "Papa? What if you used the ghost machine to help people? Like how Oliver and Gully wanted to see their dog one last time, or if someone wanted to ask for clarification on a will—things like that?"

"You have a good heart," her father said. "And if everyone in the world were more like you, then I think that would be a wonderful idea. But there are people who would take advantage of it. There are people who would be greedy, or maybe just too sad to say good-bye only once. We can't trust this secret with the world."

Emmaline was thinking of the collective look on the faces of the Sisters Allemand. The machine had helped them. It had helped Gully and Oliver, too. But it had also stolen her father away for two years.

It was a dangerous and confusing thing, that machine.

December was especially brutal this year. By the end of the first week, Emmaline, Gully, and Oliver were wading through a foot of snow on their way to school.

"Did your father get the job?" Oliver asked, rubbing his red mittens together for warmth.

"Yes," Emmaline said, and Oliver smiled at the cheer in her tone. Her bright verve this morning even coaxed a smile out of Gully's usually pensive expression. "He's starting on Monday."

It had been three days since the Sisters Allemand visited with their brother's ghost, and three days since Emmaline and her father had their conversation about living a more normal life. She had begun to write her essay and was already planning a design for its cover.

She was so happy that even the machine's ever-present humming within the house had become less of a nuisance. It was soft, automatic, like the ticking of the clocks.

"We should celebrate," Oliver said.

"The lake behind our house is frozen over," Gully said. "We could go skating."

Like the tire swing in the summer, skating in the winter was its own tradition. The twins' mother was an avid skater, and both their parents gave scuba diving lessons in the summer, and so water in all its forms was in the twins' blood. Emmaline remembered when she had first learned to skate on the DePauls' lake. She fell and slid and crashed into Gully more than she actually skated, but they'd laughed the whole time.

"Yes, let's," Emmaline said.

The school day was perfectly average, and Emmaline savored it. For lunch she ate a jelly and banana sandwich her father had made for her. The sun sat high and beaming in the winter sky, and everything about that day felt beautiful and full of hope.

After school Emmaline walked home to grab her skates from the hall closet, and she met Gully and Oliver, who were waiting for her on the log beside the lake behind their house.

Gully fixed his brother's red scarf, which had become unfurled, and Oliver swatted him away.

"I've been thinking about the ghost machine, about what I told you the other night," Oliver said to Emmaline. He didn't bother lowering his voice. The house was several yards away, and there was no one to hear them. "Have you given it any more thought?"

"Given what more thought?" Gully asked.

"I told Emmy that the machine helped the Sisters Allemand."

"So?" Gully said. "It helped them. That's no reason to allow everyone to use it."

"Not *everyone*," Oliver said. He looked past

his brother, at Emmaline. "We could decide who gets to use it. Like a test." He clapped his hands together excitedly. "We could—"

"It sounds very nice," Emmaline said. "But it would cause more problems than it would fix. They'll want more than the brief time they're given, or they won't be able to keep it a secret." Or they would just be sad all over again when the ghost left them, but she couldn't bring herself to add that out loud.

"It's too dangerous," Gully said, stepping onto the ice with an expert glide that turned into a circle.

"Just because it's dangerous doesn't mean it's a bad idea," Oliver said. "You could be very selective about who knows about it." He took Emmaline's hand, and together they pushed forward onto the ice.

"I asked my father about that, and he didn't think it was a good idea."

"There," Gully said. "See? I told you."

Oliver ignored him. He squeezed Emmaline's

hand. "I know you hate the machine sometimes, Emmy, but it can be used for good."

"It would be better if it never existed at all," Gully said, skating at Emmaline's other side. "Dead is dead."

"It doesn't have to be," Oliver said. "You never think about what it would be like to see Granny Lina's ghost?"

"Granny Lina is still alive," Gully said.

"Yes, but she's very old," Oliver said. "One day she'll die."

"That's the way things go." Gully's logic was unwavering. "And I won't want to see her as a ghost. I didn't even want to see Tidbit as a ghost, but you went behind my back after we'd agreed."

"We didn't agree," Oliver said. "You were trying to boss me around. You're always so bossy."

"I wouldn't have to be bossy if you used more sense."

"I do," Oliver said. "It's just my sense is different from yours."

Oliver and Gully often argued, and normally Emmaline didn't mind. She even found it endearing. But this argument felt more pointed somehow, and it was starting to worry her.

"Seeing a ghost is not always a good thing, Oliver," she interrupted. "I'm glad I got to speak to my mother again, but I lost a memory of her, and I can't get it back."

"But you made a new memory when you visited with her ghost," Oliver said. "And if someone I loved died, I'd make the decision to see them again."

Suddenly Emmaline was fighting the urge to cry. She had been listening to the brothers argue about the machine, and it only reminded her that there was no escaping it. Even here, where there was nothing but ice and snow, and no electricity to be seen, the machine still hummed and clattered in her brain. It haunted her just as surely as any ghost it may have produced.

She ripped her hand out of Oliver's grasp.

"You don't have to make a decision like that, because your mother is still alive. And so are your grandparents, and your family is still the way it's supposed to be."

She felt bad the instant she'd said the words. Her skates whispered to a halt, and her vision flooded with tears.

"Oh, Emmaline," Gully said. He looked at his brother. "Do you see what you did? Why can't you let things go?"

Emmaline rubbed at her eyes, and the tears caught in the fibers of her white gloves.

"I'm sorry," Oliver said. "Emmy, I didn't mean to make you sad."

She couldn't raise her head even enough to look at him.

"You're always making such a mess of things," Gully told him. He put his arm around Emmaline, and she let him guide her back to the log at the lake's edge.

They left Oliver behind, and he didn't move to follow them, guilty as he felt. He had never

made Emmaline cry before, and now he seemed afraid to say another word, like breathing too close to a house of cards about to collapse.

As soon as she sat, the tears came faster, and Emmaline buried her face in her hands.

"I really miss her, Gully," she choked out. "I wish I could have her back, and not as a ghost. I wouldn't want anyone to see someone they lost as a ghost, because it's like losing them all over again a second time, and we're not meant to lose someone twice. We're just not meant to." Her voice was strained, and as she shuddered with a sob, Gully put his arms around her.

She fell against him, and she cried like she hadn't cried in two years. She cried like the loss was brand new, because it was. Funerals ended and bodies were buried and prayers were said. But loss couldn't be buried. It could only be forgotten about for a while, during a sunny day or while listening to a pretty song, only to return anew.

Emmaline didn't know how long she cried,

but Gully didn't try to stop her. He kept his arms around her and said nothing until at last she raised her head, looked at him, and swiped the loose hair out of her eyes.

She was surprised to see that he looked as sad as she was.

"Why did he have to make that machine?" she asked him.

"I don't know," Gully said. "It isn't fair. He shouldn't have done it. I understand why you wanted to break it."

"Today started out so perfectly," she said. "I don't want to waste it by being sad."

"Maybe you needed to let it out," Gully said. "You're always trying to be happy for everyone else."

She shook her head. "I didn't mean to sound so jealous. I'm glad you and Oliver haven't lost anyone. I'm glad you don't know how this feels. You shouldn't, for a long time. And when I'm around you, I remember what it felt like to be normal."

Gully let out a small laugh. "I don't know if you'd call Oliver and me normal."

Emmaline smiled at him.

"Feeling better?" he asked.

"Yes." She rubbed at her eyes. Gully stood and held out a hand to help her to her feet, and together they shuffled their way back to the ice.

Emmaline had the thought that she should apologize to Oliver. But when she skated back onto the lake, he was gone.

"Oliver?" Gully skated under the tire swing and to the jagged rock wall that cut into the water. "Are you hiding?"

"Oliver?" Emmaline skated in a broad circle. She even looked up at the tree whose branches overlapped the lake and shielded her eyes from the sun to get a better look. Maybe he had climbed, she thought, even though she'd never known him to play hiding games before.

"Did he go back inside the house?" she asked.

"I would have seen him," Gully said. "And look. There are no footprints in the snow besides the ones we made coming out here."

Emmaline's tears were long forgotten by then, replaced by a new, slow-burning dread that made her stomach hurt.

"Oliver, this isn't funny," she said. "I'm going to be mad at you if you don't come out." That was a lofty threat. Oliver couldn't stand it when he'd made someone unhappy, and it should have brought him out immediately. But he was nowhere to be found.

Gully must have spotted something she didn't, because he skated past her so fast that the motion sent a cold breeze under her coat. She followed after him, and seconds later she saw what he did: a red scarf lying where the ice had cracked and broken, revealing a placid pool of icy water.

"Oliver!" The fear in Gully's voice made him a stranger to Emmaline. She had never seen him like this. He skated in a frenzy, and when he reached his brother's red scarf, he fell to his knees and began pulling off his skates.

"You can't," Emmaline cried. "The water's too cold. You'll drown."

But he didn't seem to hear her.

The water where the ice had broken was deceptively calm. It gave no indication that it had swallowed a boy whole, leaving nothing but an abandoned scarf.

The skates were removed, and Gully tore off his coat next. Emmaline dropped beside him and locked her arms around his a second before he would have jumped in.

"Maybe he didn't fall in!" Emmaline tried to reason. It didn't seem possible that Oliver could be down there. The day was still bright, still sunny, still carrying all the hope and promise it had this morning when she awoke. "Please, you can't go in there!" Somehow she knew that she would never see him again if he did.

But Gully was something different than the boy she knew then. He was wild, determined. He wriggled in her arms, fighting her, even elbowing her to get away. But she wouldn't let go.

Instead, Emmaline screamed. She screamed for Madame DePaul, the twins' mother, who would surely know what to do. She screamed louder than she ever had, over and over, until she saw Madame DePaul running toward them. First, there was a dishrag in her hand, and then there wasn't anything in it at all.

Gully was crying out for his brother, Emmaline realized. Maybe he'd been shouting for a while, and she had only just begun to hear him now. Her arms hurt from trying to hold him back.

"Get off the ice," Madame DePaul told him. She looked at Emmaline, her expression pleading. "Take him inside." In the next instant, Madame DePaul jumped into the water.

Gully was shaking, from the cold and from the fear, and Emmaline began to realize that this was real. Oliver had gone under while she was off sobbing about her problems. They'd left him alone, and they hadn't heard him break through.

Emmaline could see that the ice was thin where they knelt, and she thought she could hear it cracking under them.

"Gully, come on." Her voice had purpose now. She pulled him to his feet. He didn't fight her that time, and she could feel how suddenly weak he was. He was breathing hard. Both of them skidded on the ice, but somehow they didn't fall.

Madame DePaul broke through the water's surface just as Emmaline managed to lead Gully off the frozen lake.

She had Oliver held tightly in her arm, and

Emmaline went back to not believing that any of this was real. Oliver was supposed to be warm and alive, with rosy cheeks and a gentle, mischievous smile. But this boy Madame DePaul pulled from the water wasn't even breathing.

The Hospital DuMont was a very tall building ten blocks from Emmaline's house. At night she could see it from her bedroom window, its lights shining like a beacon out into the starry darkness.

She had been inside it only once, when she was born. And then she'd been swaddled in a blanket and sent home to begin her life.

Now she stepped through the glass double doors more frightened than she had ever been.

Her father was beside her, and he put his hand on her shoulder. But for the first time, she moved out of his reach. She strode to the lady at the front desk and she said, "I'm here to see Oliver DePaul. He was brought here this afternoon."

The woman at the desk smelled of berry hand sanitizer. Her hair was pulled into a high bun that Emmaline knew was yellow, and yet everything about the woman seemed black and white. The entire building seemed that way.

The woman shuffled through a stack of papers and opened a folder to read something inside. "He's on the second floor in 7B." There was sympathy in her tone, but Emmaline couldn't bring herself to acknowledge it. She didn't want to be pitied. That would mean there was something truly wrong, and she knew already that Oliver would be fine. She would find him sitting in his hospital bed, talking Gully's ears off, and when he saw her, he would pet her hair the way he always did and tell her he was sorry he'd made her sad.

She would pretend to be mad at him for making her worry. But only for a little while. And then she would hug him. And then maybe things would be in color again, rather than black and white.

"Thank you," Emmaline told the woman politely, and as she did so, she suddenly felt that manners were a waste of time.

Emmaline and her father walked toward the elevator, and after Emmaline pushed the button, she turned to her father. "Is it okay if I go alone?" she said.

Her father frowned sympathetically. He reached to pat her head, but then thought better of it and put his hands in his pockets. "I'll be right here if you need me," he said.

The elevator doors opened, and Emmaline stepped inside alone.

"Wake up," she whispered to herself after

the doors had closed. The elevator carpet was scarlet. The walls were brassy and reflective. But the girl in that reflection was a stranger, and none of the colors seemed real.

The elevator doors opened on the second floor, and when Emmaline stepped out into the hallway, suddenly it was hard to breathe.

Suddenly she was not in a hospital at all. Instead, she felt as though she were standing in the upstairs hallway of her house. She was ten years old again, and she was straining her ears to listen to the doctor and her father talking.

Somehow she knew, in that moment, that her mother was gone. She knew that there would be no more giggling and dancing across the living room, pirouetting around the coffee table and couches while music played. There would be no more pancake batter. No more kisses that her mother placed on Emmaline's nose when it crinkled as she laughed. The finality of it was certain. It filled the air

like the thick smog that erased the buildings on summer mornings.

"Wake up," she told herself again. Things were going to be different this time. Oliver was a kid, like her, and kids simply didn't die.

Emmaline walked slowly. She saw 7B ahead of her, the door open. As she got closer, she listened for the sound of Gully and Oliver bickering. Gully would be mad at his brother for making him worry, and Oliver would be saying that of course he was fine, that he was tired of being looked over and bossed around.

But as Emmaline approached, all she heard was silence. It was so silent, in fact, that she wondered if she had the right room. Her shuffling footsteps felt too loud as she stopped at the threshold.

She saw Gully first. He was sitting beside his brother's hospital bed, his head down and his back to the door so that Emmaline couldn't see his expression. Madame DePaul sat on the other side of the bed, holding Oliver's hand in both of hers. She looked very pale, and her eyes were darker than usual.

And then she saw Oliver. He was not bickering with his brother. He was not smiling. He was as white as the bed sheets, and Emmaline could see tiny purple and blue veins under his eyes. Even his hair seemed paler. His hair, usually shiny and black and full of curls, seemed gray and limp, as though it, too, were sleeping.

The next breath that Emmaline drew felt too noisy in the quiet space. Madame DePaul raised her head, and for a moment she tried to smile but couldn't. "Hello, Little *Mademoiselle* Emmaline." That was what she always called her.

Gully raised his head, and Emmaline saw his face. He and Oliver truly were twins, because he looked just as pale as his brother. The same purple and blue lines ebbed below his own eyes. He looked as though he, too, had been pulled from an icy lake. He looked so dead that it was strange to see him breathing.

"It's all right, you can come in," Madame DePaul said. Her voice sounded fragile. "We're waiting for Monsieur DePaul to return from his business trip. Lots of trains to catch, you know." She sniffled, and Emmaline braced herself. The only adult she had ever seen cry was her father, and it had been awful, and she wasn't sure that she could endure such a thing again.

But Madame DePaul didn't cry. She patted Oliver's arm and kissed his forehead.

There was a tube going into Oliver's mouth. Somehow Emmaline had not seen it until now. It made a loud, rhythmic noise that sounded more like wind than breathing. Once Emmaline became aware of it, the silence was shattered.

Her knees felt weak.

Gully looked at her for a moment, and then he looked at the floor again. He didn't even seem sad. He was something beyond sad. Worse than sad.

Emmaline heard herself whisper, "Oliver is going to be okay, isn't he?"

Madame DePaul gave Emmaline the most heartbroken smile she'd ever seen in her life. And then she said, "Come here, sweetheart."

Emmaline did, and when she stood beside Madame DePaul, Madame DePaul kissed her cheek.

Emmaline didn't know why, but this brought tears to her eyes. For the second time that day, she began to cry. The first time had been for her mother, who was already gone. But this time it was for Oliver, who was not supposed to be gone for a very long time. She had never thought to worry about losing Oliver, or Gully; it hadn't seemed possible. It still didn't.

Madame DePaul put her arms around her, and that made the tears come even harder, because Madame DePaul had to let go of her son's hand to do it, and Emmaline didn't think she deserved to be the reason Madame DePaul let go of Oliver even for a second. This was all her fault. If she hadn't gone off to sulk, she and Gully would have seen him fall through. They would have grabbed his hands and pulled him to the surface. Gully would have scolded him. "You have to be more careful," he'd have said, and Oliver would have rolled his eyes and said, "Stop being so bossy."

But Gully and Oliver weren't arguing now. There was only the stillness of the hospital room, and the soft sound of tears, and the machine that made Oliver breathe. That machine was just like the ghost machine in the basement. It gave the illusion of a living thing, but an illusion was all it was.

Gully didn't cry. His mouth was pressed into a tight line, and he stared at his brother's face the same way he stared at his books. The same way he stared at math problems, and at science lab experiments, and any other thing that needed to be solved.

Emmaline couldn't bear it. She stepped out of Madame DePaul's comforting embrace. She stepped away from the hospital bed.

Through her watery, blurred vision, she looked at Oliver. She looked at him and looked at him, as though that alone could force him to wake up. She couldn't believe that this was real, but it didn't seem to matter what she believed.

She had expected him to be feeling better when she visited him. She had expected him to pet her hair and tell her he was sorry for making her cry on the lake. But instead, she was the one who said, "I'm sorry, Oliver." Her voice was broken and squeaky. "I'm sorry."

At the sound of her voice, Gully squeezed his eyes shut. His shoulders were quivering.

Emmaline ran before she knew she was moving. She ran out of the room and down the hall, and she was gasping by the time she stepped inside the elevator.

The elevator doors closed. She wiped furiously at her eyes. *Stop crying*, she told herself. Crying would make it true. But if she didn't cry, like Gully and Madame DePaul, then soon Oliver would be better and there would be nothing to cry about at all.

Chapter 11

That night, the Beaumont house was quiet except for the humming of the machine. Emmaline ran straight to her bedroom as soon as they had returned from the hospital and slammed the door so hard it shook the walls.

That was four hours ago. Julien knew this because he had gotten better at paying attention to clocks. For Emmaline's sake, he was being more mindful of the living world and all its rules.

For the first three hours since their return,

he'd cleaned the house. He vacuumed the rug in the living room, and he scrubbed the sink, and he dusted the window ledges and the mantel. He watered the little pink flower that Emmaline had brought home and managed to keep alive through the fall.

And then, for the fourth hour, he sat on the basement steps, staring at his machine. He held his wife's blue silk scarf in his hands. It still smelled of her perfume, and he could still remember the elegant way she'd draped it around her neck as she would study herself in the hall mirror before going out.

"I miss you desperately," he told her, although she wasn't there to hear it. "Our Emmaline is hurting, Margeaux. What do I do?"

But at the end of the hour, when the clock struck eleven, he still hadn't put the scarf in the machine. He couldn't relinquish the memory of his wife smiling at him as she opened the door on their way out to a party. There were so many memories attached to that scarf. He didn't know which he would lose, but he couldn't bear to part with any of them.

Instead of summoning his wife's ghost, he returned the scarf to the hall closet, and he went to check on Emmaline, who was still very much alive.

He knocked on the door. "Emmaline? Can I bring you some dinner? You should eat something."

After several seconds, her small voice answered, "I'm not hungry."

"Can I come in?"

She sniffled. "All right."

Emmaline was sitting curled up on her window ledge, staring at the hospital across town. Rivers of tears were drying on her cheeks.

Julien pulled the chair away from Emmaline's desk and sat beside her. "Do you want to talk about it?"

Emmaline took a shaky breath. "We were talking about the machine the last time I spoke to him." Her voice was hoarse and spent from hours of sobbing. "He said something that made me upset, and then he told me that he was sorry. But I didn't answer him. I skated away, and left him alone. I wanted him to feel bad. I was jealous that his mother was still alive." She didn't fully realize this was true until she'd said it out loud, and it brought a new sort of pain. She had wanted Oliver to feel bad. Oliver, who would do anything in the world to make her happy.

She hugged her knees tighter. "I want to tell him that it's okay and I'm not mad at him. I want to tell him I'm sorry for being so awful."

Julien couldn't bear the sight of his daughter's tears. Loss was never fair. Death was most always an injustice; everyone came into the world with the hope that they would live to be very old. Not everyone would. But in the case of children, it was especially cruel.

"Oliver has always been very observant," Julien said. "That's a gift, you know, to be able to read people so well. Few people are good at that."

Emmaline looked at him, her eyes pink and swollen.

"And I'm sure he knew everything you just told me," Julien went on. "He understood why you were upset, and he knew that you would be back to yourself again in a little while."

Emmaline shook her head. "I shouldn't have left him. He never would have left me."

"Oliver knows that you care about him very much," Julien said.

"I just want to tell him." Emmaline's voice was tiny and high pitched. "I haven't ever told him how much I care about him."

"That's because it went without saying," Julien said. "There are some people who mean so much to you, even if you never tell them, you both just know it."

Emmaline looked at the hospital again. She was wondering if Monsieur DePaul had taken all the trains and buses that would lead him to

Oliver's bedside. She was wondering what would happen once he arrived.

"I should have told him," she said.

Emmaline lay in bed for hours, staring at the hospital lights in the distance. Her mind was filled with all the things she wished she had said when she had the chance. When she closed her eyes, she saw the words swirling and swirling like water going down a drain, and she couldn't catch them before they slipped away forever.

The sun had begun to rise by the time she fell asleep.

Not long after that, the phone rang.

"Emmaline?" She awoke to the sound of her bedroom door creaking open. She opened her eyes and saw her father standing in the hallway, but she didn't move. His expression made her afraid to. She knew too well what bad news looked like even before it was said.

"Emmaline, I've just gotten a call from Madame DePaul. She'd like for you to come and see Oliver, to tell him good-bye."

Emmaline had thought she had run dry of tears, but there always seemed to be more. Her body curled in on itself. "No," she whimpered. Her body shook. She felt cold and sick.

This time yesterday, Oliver had been waking up in his own bed, across the room from Gully. He got up, and brushed his teeth, and combed his hair, and went out into the world as though he had a hundred more years to live. But he hadn't even had one more day.

Her father sat on the edge of the bed. He tried to touch her shoulder, but she pulled away from him. She covered her face with her hands and screamed. She screamed the way she had screamed for Madame DePaul when Oliver was underwater and Gully tried to go after him. She screamed the way she had wanted to scream when they buried her mother, but she had been too timid and stunned, standing there in her black lace dress under the baking sun.

She screamed for Oliver to come back.

And then, after she was through, she got up, because that was what always came next, no matter what.

She walked to the hospital, her father at her side. The entire morning felt unreal. It had snowed in the night, coating the city in a fresh sheet of white that glinted and winked in the early sunlight. The sky was pink, like Oliver's rosy cheeks.

Her fists clenched in her pockets.

This time, when she entered the hospital elevator, Emmaline told herself that she was prepared for what awaited her in room 7B. She stared at her own dulled reflection in the brass doors, until they slid open and revealed the hallway like a yawning mouth.

But even though she had prepared herself, the fear and the sadness overtook her anew,

and the elevator doors had begun to close by the time she mustered the courage to step forward.

Oliver was still in his bed, and the tube was still in his mouth. Gully was still beside him. Monsieur and Madame DePaul were standing over both of their children, and their eyes were red and swollen.

"Emmaline." Madame DePaul tried to smile, but she cried instead.

"Gully?" Emmaline whispered. He didn't look at her, but he reached for her hand. He was wearing two scarves draped over his neck: one green and one red.

She let him take her hand—the left hand, on which she wore her black lace glove—and she could feel that he was shaking.

Oliver was very still, aside from the way his chest rose and fell as air was forced through the tube.

Gully leaned close and whispered in her ear, "I told them to wait for you."

Emmaline didn't know what to say. If they

had waited for her, she wished she'd taken more time walking here. She wished she had sailed around the world and back again first, just to keep air in Oliver's lungs.

"Oliver is gone," Madame DePaul said, and there was a wave of tears beating against the door of her words, trying to flood her. "And we have to say good-bye now."

Good-bye. Emmaline had said the word a thousand times. Good-bye to the mailman after he'd delivered the mail, good-bye to her father as she left for school, good-bye to Gully, good-bye to Oliver, good-bye when she hung up the phone. But now the word felt like a mountain to climb, filled with monsters and fires. Good-bye felt impossible and cruel.

She leaned forward and touched Oliver's hair. It was soft and warm, even though his face was white and still. His hair still smelled like him, she realized. His wool coat and his house and the pie-scented candles that his mother always had burning in the kitchen.

All night her mind had been filled with the things she wished she had said to him while he could hear her, but now she couldn't think of a single one. They'd all gone down the drain that led to an ocean too vast to search.

She wasn't even sure if her heart was still beating. She couldn't feel it in her chest.

Still holding on to her hand, Gully leaned forward and kissed his brother's forehead. Emmaline had never seen him do that. "I love you," he whispered. "I love you, I love you." Emmaline had never heard him say that, either. Gully had said so many things to his brother—maybe this was the only thing left that he hadn't.

Gully was holding tight to her hand, as though she would leave him if he didn't. Maybe she would have. She was finding it very difficult to breathe in this room, and very difficult not to run outside, where everything was covered by snow and time didn't seem to exist and there were no good-byes to say.

But she stayed. She listened to Monsieur

and Madame DePaul whisper their good-byes, even though her mind had grown hazy and she couldn't understand the words they were saying. She stayed when the doctor came. She stayed as the machine was turned off. She stayed and watched as Oliver put up no fight to live, because there was nothing left of him. Nothing but organs and skin and bones he had already abandoned, because they had failed to hold him. The whole world itself failed to hold him. She stayed even after his last breath was gone.

In the silence that followed that last breath, Gully drew a breath of his own. The first breath to begin a lifetime without a twin. It looked like it hurt him, Emmaline thought.

Madame DePaul was the first to break down. She crumpled and collapsed and wailed, and Monsieur DePaul caught her.

Gully let go of Emmaline's hand, and before she could even turn to face him, he had run from the room.

She chased after him, but he was already gone by the time she'd reached the hallway. All that was left was the sound of Madame DePaul crying, and the nothingness where Oliver had once been.

Chapter 12

Emmaline didn't get out of bed the next day. It was a Friday, but Julien didn't remind her that she had school. He knocked on her door in the morning, and again when the clock struck twelve, and both times she didn't answer. When he opened the door to check on her, she pulled the blankets over her head and rolled away from him.

He had never seen her like this.

When Emmaline's mother died, that had been a grief she and Julien shared. They salted their tea with their tears and they shared memories. But Oliver was different. Children were the promise that life was long, and that it went on no matter how ugly and unfair it sometimes seemed.

Julien did not try to offer his daughter some words to make sense of this. She was a smart-enough girl, and she knew more about it than anyone her age should. She knew that there was no sense to be made.

The black lace dress that Emmaline had worn to her mother's funeral no longer fit. Time had passed since then, and the pain had scabbed over, only to be torn wide open again with brand-new loss. The dress wasn't supposed to fit anymore, and there wasn't supposed to be another funeral.

She took her red dress from the hanger. Oliver's favorite color. She put a matching headband in her hair.

It was Sunday, and so cold that it seeped through Emmaline's wool coat. She felt that chill even as she entered the warmth of the church.

"Do you want to sit up front with the DePauls?" her father asked.

Emmaline shook her head. She felt so weak. Even from the door, she could see Gully in the front pew, seated between his mother and father. There was an empty space beside him, as though the DePauls didn't know how to be three; they only knew how to make room for four.

There were so many people in the church whom Emmaline had never met. Aunts, cousins, friends of the DePauls, and some classmates. Emmaline didn't look closely at any of them. She stared at her hands, and her black lace glove, which she now wore for both her mother and Oliver.

When the prayers had been muttered and words had been spoken, Emmaline could not get outside fast enough. She ran out into the December air and down the church steps and all the way to the street before she realized that she had nowhere to go. Roads were splayed out before her, and they could take her anywhere in the world, but she didn't know where to go.

She stood there for a very long time, gasping, the wind freezing the tears so that they didn't fall. She was grateful for that. She was tired of crying.

The church doors opened, and some of the mourners stepped outside, while others stayed. Emmaline didn't know how anyone could stay inside the church. Not with Oliver's body inside a small white coffin with roses on the lid.

She turned to face the doors, and she saw her father coming toward her. She hoped that Gully would be behind him. That he would come and try to make sense of all this. He was so good at that. He knew how many seconds it took to walk through the city, and how many stairs were in the school, and what time the sun rose and set depending on the day.

But she couldn't find him in the crowd.

A week passed. Emmaline dialed the DePauls' number every day, and the line was busy every time. Either there were well-wishers calling, or they had taken the phone off the hook.

On the eighth day after the funeral, Emmaline waded through the snow and made her way to Gully and Oliver's house. It had been three whole days since she'd cried, and she was hoping to make today the fourth, if she could bear it.

Madame DePaul was the one to answer the door. She was wearing a long robe and her eyes were misty, but she smiled. The house was dark behind her, the curtains drawn and the radio playing softly. "Hello, Little Mademoiselle Emmaline," she said.

Emmaline knew what it was like for a child who lost a mother, but she had never seen a

mother who lost a child. Somehow she knew that Madame DePaul's sadness was even deeper and darker than her own.

"Hi." Emmaline's voice was soft. "Is Gully home?"

The question felt strange. She had never had to ask before. Usually one of the twins came to the door and let her in. And even when Emmaline called, she never asked for just one of them. She would say, "Is Gully or Oliver there?"

Madame DePaul opened the door wider to let her in. "He's up in his bedroom," she said. "I know he'll be glad to see you. Just—be patient with him."

Emmaline practically tiptoed up the stairs. The calm within the house felt so tentative, as though one creaky floorboard would cause the entire building to collapse.

Gully and Oliver's bedroom door was closed, and she knocked softly. "Gully? It's me. It's Emmy."

There was the sound of shuffling on the other side, and then Gully opened the door. He still looked pale and strange, but a bit more like himself than the last time she'd seen him.

"Can I come in?" she asked.

"No," he said. "I'd like you to leave."

Her heart ached at that. "Why?"

"Because I don't want anything to do with that machine."

"Well, I haven't brought it with me," Emmaline said. "See?" She turned her pockets inside out, hoping to coax a smile out of him. It didn't work. "And I didn't come to talk to you about that, Gully. Not at all."

"It doesn't matter. If I think about you, I think about . . . that thing. And I don't trust myself. I don't trust that I . . ." His voice trailed. It wasn't like him to struggle with words.

"You're afraid you'll be tempted to use my father's machine," Emmaline said, understanding.

He stared at her for a long and painful

moment, then nodded. "I don't want to lose a single memory of Oliver. Not a single one."

"Then I won't allow you to ask to use it," she said. "If you even try to ask, if you even say the *word* 'machine,' I'll slap you."

That made him laugh. And then as soon as the sound came out, his hand flew up to cover his mouth, as though this was forbidden. As though he should not be allowed to laugh so soon after his brother's death.

"Please let me in," Emmaline said. "I've really missed you."

Gully stepped aside to make room for her.

The room looked the same as it always had. Small and tidy, with two beds separated by a tall window that revealed a landscape of snow. Oliver's bed was rumpled and unmade. Professor Rêver, Oliver's teddy bear, was tossed against the blankets, presumably where Oliver had left him.

Gully's bed was also unmade, which was very peculiar, and Emmaline realized that he must have been spending his days in it. The twins' bedroom overlooked the lake in the yard, and Emmaline worried for Gully. Knowing him, he was looking at that lake and the footprints that led out to it every day. He was remembering every detail.

"Do you want to go for a walk?" Emmaline said.

"It's too cold," he replied. Usually he liked the cold. But now he returned to his bed and lay on top of the unmade covers and curled onto his side. Away from her.

"Do you want to talk about your memories?" she tried hesitantly. "Since you've decided to keep them all."

Gully didn't answer, and since he hadn't invited Emmaline to sit, she stood between the two beds. "I have one," she went on. "I remember when Oliver fell out of the tree in the school yard because he'd wanted to get a look at the bird nest we'd spotted there. He landed in the rosebush and one of the thorns cut him under his left eye, and it ended up leaving a scar. He didn't even mind—do you remember?—because now that he had a scar, people wouldn't always get the two of you confused."

Emmaline blinked and found herself standing in the twins' bedroom. The memory had felt so real that for a moment she'd forgotten it had happened such a long time ago.

Oliver's teddy bear stared at her with great interest. Gully curled up tighter. "It was kind of you to stop by, but you should go now."

"Gully—"

"Go." His tone was sharp, and Emmaline went rigid, feeling as though she'd just been slapped.

She saw Gully reach under his pillow and gather something into his arms. Something red. Oliver's scarf. He held on tightly, but a scarf was not a person, and his arms were filled with so much empty space.

"Oh, Gully." She walked closer to his bed. Her hand hovered over his shoulder, but she didn't touch him. She wanted him to know that she was there, and if he needed to hold on to someone, he could hold on to her. But she couldn't get the words out.

He buried his face in the scarf. "Go away, Emmaline. I don't want to see you anymore."

Her throat was dry. "Not ever?"

He turned onto his stomach and pulled the blankets over his head. "Don't come back here. I can't be your friend anymore."

"Because of the machine?" The words sounded breathless. "Gully, I wasn't going to use it. I wouldn't."

"Go away." His voice broke.

A bit of the red scarf still peeked out from under the blankets. Emmaline imagined the scarf falling into the machine. She imagined losing that memory of Oliver being pulled from the ice. There would be a black space in her mind where that awful image had been. And in exchange, she would get to spend a few seconds with Oliver again. She would get to see his sweet smile and hold his hands and tell him that she loved him. That was what she should have said to him in the hospital, but she'd been unable to think clearly.

Oliver. She looked to his bed. He was gone. He wasn't going to come home. She would do anything to bring him back, even for one minute.

No, she told herself. Not anything.

Emmaline ran the entire way home. She ran through the front door and barreled through the kitchen, past her father, who was making tea at the stove, and a bouquet of flowers and a card that someone had sent along with their condolences. She ran down the basement steps, and it seemed as though the house shook from the weight of her footsteps.

She ran until she reached the machine, and

then she stared at it, gasping, her teeth gritted and fists clenched. She kicked it. It didn't even dent. She kicked it again, harder that time, and then began hitting it with her fists.

"Emmaline!" Her father was pulling her away, but she was still trying to kick at the machine. She was grunting and shouting that she hated it, that it had ruined everything, that she should have done a better job destroying it the first time she'd tried.

"Emmaline. Emmaline!" Her father did not let go of her until she had exhausted herself. And then he grabbed her shoulders and knelt down to face her. There were tears in her eyes by then, and her entire face was red. She swiped at her runny nose. "What is this about?" he said.

"'What is this about?'" she bit back. "Oliver is dead. We had to let go of Oliver forever, and you can't even let go of a machine. You won't even unplug it."

"If I unplug the machine, I don't know what that will do," her father said. "It may change things. It may mean that it never works again."

"Good!" Emmaline sobbed. "It's ruined everything. It's ruined all our lives."

Her father frowned. He brushed away her tears with his thumb and said, "You don't want to see Oliver right now, but someday that may change. It could be years from now, when you feel like you need him."

"You think I don't *want* to see Oliver?" Her voice was tight with tears and anger. "I want to see him every day. I need him every day. But he's gone. I can't have him back."

"Emmaline—"

"Please unplug the machine, Papa," she croaked. "Before it takes away anything else. *Please.*"

"You know I can't do that, Emmy."

"Of course you can't." She shook her head. "You'll never do it. But if I die, *don't* try to bring me back. I don't want anything to do with that thing. I don't want anything to do with *you*."

Before she could register her father's wounded expression, she hurried back up the stairs. She couldn't be in this house anymore. Every room held the humming of the ghost machine, and she was so tired of hearing it.

She went back outside into the cold afternoon air.

Once again, she realized that she didn't know where she was going. The only ones who could comfort her now were either dead, or had told her to go away.

Chapter 13

It was well past midnight when Gully heard the knock at the door. He hadn't been sleeping, and now he sat up in bed.

There was a nervous feeling in his stomach. Nobody came to the door this late unless it was important, and with Oliver gone, what could possibly be important?

He climbed out of bed and stood at the top of the stairs. For a few seconds, he thought that somehow it would be Oliver. That the hospital had made a mistake, and he wasn't dead at all.

But when Gully's father answered the door, with his mother behind him, he saw Emmaline's father standing on the front steps. His hair was disheveled, his face more serious than it had ever been.

"I'm sorry to call on you so late at night," Monsieur Beaumont said, "but I was hoping Emmaline would be here. She hasn't come home."

Gully began walking down the stairs, and he moved slowly, as though afraid of what would happen when he reached the last step. "Emmaline is gone?"

Gully's parents turned to face him. His mother pushed some of the messy curls from his forehead. "Gully?" she said. "Do you know where Emmaline could be?"

Even though it was illogical, Gully imagined Emmaline falling through the ice, too. His chest felt tight. "She was here this afternoon."

Monsieur Beaumont was looking at Gully

as though Gully held all the hope in the world. "Did she say anything? Anything at all?"

It hurt to breathe, suddenly. "She invited me to go for a walk." He looked helplessly between his mother and father, too ashamed to look at Monsieur Beaumont. "I told her I didn't want to be her friend anymore. I told her to leave. I—I thought she would just go home."

Even now, telling the story, he didn't recognize the boy who had said such a thing. He was surprised that he could even be so cruel. "I didn't mean it," he said.

"It's all right, Gully, it's all right," his mother said. He doubted there was anything in the world he could do to make her scold him now that Oliver was gone. "Can you think about where she'd be?"

Gully didn't answer, because he was already hurrying toward the back door. Even without bothering to grab his coat, he ran into the yard.

The moonlight cast a sheen across the snow. The footsteps were all still there: His and

Oliver's coming from the back door out into the frozen lake, and Emmaline's coming from the side gate when she'd joined them. And his mother's tracks as she ran when Emmaline screamed for her. And beside those, the mess of footsteps all crossing into one another as they'd scrambled back to the house: his and his mother's and Emmaline's (who had still been wearing her skates), but not Oliver's.

No one had been in the yard since the day Oliver drowned. He knew this. There was proof. But logic had not been as reliable as he'd once believed. There were ghosts in machines and memories that disappeared, and if those things were possible, then it was also possible that Emmaline was trapped under the ice.

He ran across the yard, creating a fresh set of tracks. He heard his parents calling for him, but their voices felt miles away.

He made it all the way to the edge of the lake, and he stopped, gasping. The cold air stabbed at his lungs. He saw the hole where the ice had been too weak, and Oliver had fallen through so suddenly that he didn't even get the chance to call for help before he went under.

The water was black and bottomless, and from where he stood, he looked for Emmaline's light hair. Her white gloves.

For some reason, he couldn't move.

Arms wrapped around him. Someone draped a coat over his shoulders. "What is it?" his mother said. She couldn't bring herself to look at the lake; she had even closed the curtain of the kitchen window that overlooked it.

Logic came flooding back. Not everything he lost would turn up under the ice.

"Emmaline isn't here." His voice was broken. "I don't know where she is."

By the time the sun came up, Emmaline's father had phoned the police. He felt as though a hand had reached through the sky and torn the breath from his lungs.

Madame and Monsieur DePaul had been searching for hours. They searched the school, and the trees, and the graveyard where Emmaline's mother, and now Oliver, were buried.

Gully climbed trees for a better vantage point. He even knocked on all the neighbors' doors—even the ones who didn't like children and had told Emmaline more than once to keep to the sidewalk and stop cutting across their lawns.

By himself, he went to the grave of Emmaline's mother, and then, steeling himself, he went to Oliver's. He knew that this, too, was illogical, but he'd always gone to Oliver when he needed help. He didn't know where else to turn.

"Please let her be all right," he said, even though he knew he was only talking to a stone with his brother's name engraved onto it. "I did something awful, Oliver, and I need to fix it."

The stone with Oliver's name on it didn't answer. It couldn't. Oliver existed only in memories now. The memory that haunted Gully the most as of late was of visiting Oliver in the hospital, with its shiny floors and somber rooms. After Oliver was gone—really, truly gone, and no longer breathing—he'd run through the hospital trying to get away from that feeling of death and stillness. As he ran, he'd been thinking, *If Oliver were with me, where would he want to go?*

That was when he'd smelled something that reminded him, just a little bit, of the pie-scented candles his mother burned in the kitchen. He'd followed it and found what turned out to be a tray of fresh pastries in the hospital cafeteria. It was the only room filled with people who were talking and moving as though they were still alive and still had hope. In that moment, he'd needed hope more than anything.

The shortest Allemand sister was the one who found Emmaline, and she hadn't even been looking for her. She hadn't even known that Emmaline was missing.

Emmaline was sitting in the hospital cafeteria, staring at the people who came and went. They bought coffee and tea, and sometimes stale-looking bread and sweets. She wondered if the people they were visiting would get better. She hoped that they would.

The shortest Allemand sister had come to the cafeteria for coffee (black with ten sugars), and she was just about to take a table alone by the window when she spotted the little Beaumont girl staring off into space. "What are you doing here?" the shortest Allemand sister asked her. "Is someone sick? Is it your father?"

Emmaline looked startled, as though she'd just been jarred out of a dream. "Huh?" Her vacant tone was most uncharacteristic of the bright and clever girl she was. "Oh. No. I'm not visiting anyone. I'm just watching." She blinked as Mademoiselle Allemand sat across from her. "Why are you at the hospital?"

"Edith has an early appointment with her doctor."

"Edith?" Emmaline asked.

The shortest Allemand sister smiled. "That's my sister. The tall one."

Emmaline had lived across the street from the sisters all her life, and now she realized that she had never learned any of their names.

"I'm Gretchen," the shortest sister said. "Our other sister is Agnes."

Emmaline tried to smile. "I hope your sister feels better."

"Well, she is very old," Mademoiselle Allemand said. "Not young like Agnes and me." She laughed at her own joke.

Emmaline should have laughed. It was the polite thing to do. But her heart was hurting and she couldn't muster it. "My friend Oliver was supposed to grow old," she said. "He wanted to grow so old that he could hardly walk without a cane, and then he wanted to use the ghost machine one more time, to say hello after a lifetime of good-byes. He thought that would be nice."

"Ah, yes, I heard about the little DePaul boy," Mademoiselle Allemand said. "I know how close you were. I sent you flowers."

"Thank you," Emmaline said. "I'm sure they're lovely, but I haven't seen them yet. I haven't been home for a while."

"No?" Mademoiselle Allemand said. "Isn't your father worried about you?"

Emmaline shook her head. "He doesn't notice me. All he thinks about is his machine, and bringing my mother back."

"We all have to say good-bye at some point," Mademoiselle Allemand said. "But it's harder for some than others."

"Yes, but we have to say it," Emmaline said. "My father refuses to."

Mademoiselle Allemand put her hand on top of Emmaline's, and Emmaline was surprised at how soft it was. Her many rings were cool against Emmaline's skin. "Edith isn't going to

get better," she said. "She's been sick for quite a while, and we've been lucky to have her around for as long as we have, but her doctor tells us that this will be her last New Year."

"Oh." Emmaline's voice softened. "I'm sorry."

"There's nothing to be sorry about," Mademoiselle Allemand said. "She's had a very long life, and thanks to you, she was able to see our dear Granville one more time."

Emmaline considered. "It wasn't painful to see him again? It didn't confuse you?"

"Death is always confusing," Mademoiselle Allemand said. "And it's always painful. But what your friend Oliver said was true. It was very nice to say hello and good-bye. Granville died many years ago, and we got to tell him some of the things he had missed. We told him about his granddaughter, who has his eyes, and that his wife still dances to their favorite song."

"And that was enough?" Emmaline said. "You don't want to see him over and over again?"

"Once was enough," Mademoiselle Allemand said. "It's more than most people get."

Emmaline looked up. The morning windows were full of sun, so bright as it reflected off of the white and the ice. She could almost believe that Oliver was out there in a heaven made of snow. But then she began to make out the edges of buildings, and the people walking through the streets. None of those people were him.

"I'm very glad that the machine could help you," Emmaline said. "But I think it's long past time for it to be put away."

"Emmaline!" Gully was running through the doorway, and his volume attracted more than a few chiding stares from nearby adults.

Emmaline stood, and before she could say a word, he had pulled her into a hug so tight that her feet rose from the ground for a second. "Where have you been?" He drew back and held her by her forearms. "We've been out looking for you all night."

She blinked. "You have?"

"Of course," he cried. "You can't just disappear like that."

"But you said you didn't want to be my friend anymore. I thought—"

"I was acting stupid. I felt guilty, because seeing you yesterday made me feel better, and I don't have any right to be happy without Oliver." There was so much pain on his face. He was no longer pale. There were no longer veins under his eyes. He no longer resembled Oliver after he'd been pulled from the ice. And Emmaline understood how much this must have hurt him, to see himself in the mirror and know that he was left to live on. "I'm sorry," he said.

Emmaline threw her arms around him, and he held on just as tightly. "I'm sorry, too," she said. "I'm sorry about the machine. I'm sorry I led us off of the ice. I'm sorry for all of it."

When Emmaline thought to look to Mademoiselle Allemand to tell her good-bye, she found that Mademoiselle Allemand was gone.

"You shouldn't be sorry," Gully said. "I'm

the one who said we should go skating. It was my fault. And then I scolded him, and that was the last thing I ever got to say to him. I think about it the second I wake up, and it never goes away."

When they finally let go of each other, Emmaline petted his cheek, the way that Oliver would have. And it was like he was there with them. "You *do* deserve to be happy, Gully. He wouldn't want us to blame ourselves."

"No." Gully sniffled. "He would want us to make flower crowns and dance all the way home like carnival clowns."

Emmaline laughed. "Well," she said, "there are no flowers left on the ground, but there is plenty of room for us to dance."

Chapter 14

When Emmaline and Gully returned to her house, Emmaline's father knelt to her height and gathered her into his arms even before she was able to unbutton her coat. "Never do that again." His voice was muffled as he held on to her. "Never, never do that again."

"I didn't think you would notice I was gone," Emmaline said. It was the truth, and now she felt guilty to know that she had been wrong.

Madame and Monsieur DePaul were there, and they pulled Gully close, grateful still for the child who was able to come home to them.

While Emmaline and her father were still holding tight to each other, the DePauls left quietly and closed the door behind them.

"What were you thinking, staying out all night like that?" Emmaline's father didn't sound angry, though. He sounded relieved. "Where were you?"

"I went to the hospital," Emmaline said. "I wanted to see that sometimes people get better. It feels like everyone I care about is dying. It feels like all anyone ever wants to talk to me about is ghosts."

Emmaline's father looked at her. "We have talked about ghosts a lot, haven't we?" he said. "But I thought that you would want to see Oliver again, even if it was as a ghost. And maybe Gully would, too, once you'd had the time to think about it. I didn't tell Madame and Monsieur DePaul that the machine is working, but one day, I thought you might like for them to know."

Emmaline shook her head. "I don't want to see him as a ghost. I want to remember what he was like while he was alive." A stab of pain in her chest surprised her. No matter how many times she reminded herself that Oliver was no longer alive, it never got easier. "Gully said that he didn't want to be my friend anymore, because he was so afraid that he'd be tempted to use the machine. And—I—I wish you would just turn it off. I listen to it humming and it almost makes me forget that memories are more important than ghosts."

Her father smiled sadly. "Okay, Emmy."

He stood, and she looked up at him, confused. "Okay?"

Her father went to the hall closet, and he took the scarf that had belonged to Emmaline's mother off of its hook. "Come with me," he said. "I want to tell you something."

He opened the basement door, and Emmaline followed him.

The machine was still emitting its purple glow, humming against the basement wall. For a thing made almost entirely out of scrap metal and spare parts and rusty screws, it was surprisingly indestructible. There were no dents or scuffs from where Emmaline had attacked it the night before.

Emmaline stopped halfway down the stairs, her heart caught in her mouth. That machine could bring Oliver back. She knew that, of course, but now it really hit her. That machine would allow her to see him, even hug him. All the things she wished she had said to him came rushing through her mind:

I'm sorry I stormed off to feel sorry for myself, Oliver. I was just jealous.

You've always made me see the good in things, and I'll remember that for the rest of my life.

I love you.

She took a deep breath, and descended the rest of the stairs.

Her father sat on the bottom step, and Emmaline took the space beside him. He was holding the silk scarf in his hands, and the perfume was still strong enough that Emmaline could almost believe her mother was there beside them.

"The first month after you were born," her father said, "we didn't know what we were doing. It seemed like we got everything wrong, and all we managed to do was make you cry."

"Really?" Emmaline said.

"One night, it was raining pretty heavily. It was windy, and the electricity went out, and we couldn't find the candles. The thunder woke you, and you started to cry. You cried and cried and just wouldn't stop. Your mother sat down in the rocking chair with you in her arms, and she started crying, too."

The idea of a baby making an adult cry was so absurd that Emmaline giggled. "Did you cry, too?"

Emmaline's father laughed. "I wanted to. We felt like such awful parents. We couldn't even find the candles—how were we going to take care of a baby if we couldn't even get some light in the room? That was what we were thinking."

"You were great parents," Emmaline said, still laughing just a little. "And the candles are under the kitchen sink."

"Well, now they are," her father said. "Back then we didn't have anything organized. We learned that as we went. And that night we couldn't find the candles, we also ran out of diapers."

Emmaline was trying not to laugh anymore, but the idea of her parents scrambling so frantically to take care of her was funny, because it didn't sound like them at all. They had always seemed to know just what they were doing—before the machine was invented, that is.

"So I went out in the rain and the wind, and I walked to the store on the corner to buy diapers," her father said. "It was the only place still open so late at night."

"Belgarde's?" Emmaline asked.

"Yes, Belgarde's. You know how they sell little trinkets by the pharmacy. Earrings and wind-up toys and things. And that night, I saw a display of silk scarves. This one reminded me of her eyes. It was such a small, silly thing, but I thought maybe it would cheer her up."

Emmaline smiled at that. "Did it?"

"More than I could have imagined," he said. "She kept it for the rest of her life. She wore it to parties, and to dinners, and when we went for long walks in the evenings."

"I remember that," Emmaline said.

Her father sighed, and his expression became melancholy. "This scarf holds a lot of memories."

"They're good ones," Emmaline said. "That one you just told me—it was nice. I didn't know about it."

Her father looked at the machine, glowing in his wife's favorite shade of purple.

"Do you want to see her again?" he asked.

Emmaline put her hand on his. "I just did," she said. "In that story you told me. I want to see her again that way."

"I do have lots of stories," he said.

"Maybe you could tell them to me more often," Emmaline said.

When her father looked at her, she could see that something had changed. "When I couldn't find you last night, I wasn't even thinking about the machine. It was the first time in two years that it didn't matter to me at all."

"I'm sorry, Papa. I didn't mean to make you worry."

"It was for the best," he said. "I don't need ghosts. I have my memories, and I have you."

Emmaline felt hope bubble up in her chest. "Is it time to unplug the machine?"

"Yes," he said. "It's time."

Together, they stood and walked to the machine. Its hum was louder from behind, and Emmaline felt a warm gust of air from all the electricity and the metal fans working to keep the circuits from overheating. There were more than a dozen plugs connected to extension cords tangled together, all of which led to a single plug in the wall.

Julien stooped and unplugged the machine.

The basement turned dark, save for the thin cracks of sunlight streaming in through the covered window.

Emmaline dragged the chair to the window so that she could reach the cardboard barricading it and let in the morning sun.

The house was so quiet. Quieter than it had been in two years. There was no machine to work on. No clatter of tools. No humming of circuits or clanging of gears. There was only the world, and everything still alive within it.

CHAPTER 15

Gully didn't return to school the following week, but when Emmaline walked past his house, she would look to the living room window and find him waiting for her. He would raise his hand and uncurl his fingers one at a time in a little wave. He couldn't quite bring himself to smile, though she could see that he was considering it.

On Saturday, when she came to see him, Gully wouldn't come to the door. "He just can't seem to move today," Madame DePaul said. "Come back tomorrow. Maybe then."

On Sunday, when Emmaline came back, she convinced him to get out of bed and go for a walk. "You don't even have to change out of your pajamas or brush your hair," she said. "I don't mind." And so he wore his pinstriped pajamas and his gray wool slippers as he followed her outside. He was also wearing both scarves—the red and the green—and he didn't say anything as they began walking toward the café.

Emmaline noted the familiar studiousness coming out behind the sorrow in his expression, and she knew that he was counting the seconds between the sidewalk cracks.

"How much longer until we get there?" she asked him.

"At this pace, only one more minute."

They lapsed back into silence. He was having a very hard time, Emmaline knew, and she didn't want to scare him off. Or worse, make him cry. She felt as though they were walking on a tightrope, and one wrong step would cause it to snap, and they'd both fall into a bottomless pit.

She let him go on counting.

Gully stopped when they reached the café. His breaths were coming out a little faster, sending bursts of white into the cold air. Breaths he took without Oliver there to match them.

"Do you think it's all right," he finally said, "to go inside? Without him?"

Emmaline realized in that moment that she'd expected Oliver to be waiting for them at a table by the window. Some piece of her was still trying to find him, as though he kept turning the corners too fast for her to reach him, but one day she would catch up.

"Are you worried he'd feel left out?" she asked.

Gully pressed his lips together, the way he did when he was analyzing something. "I don't know." His voice cracked. "I always knew everything about him, but I've never been apart

from him for this long, so I don't know what he would want me to do anymore."

Emmaline touched his shoulder, carefully.

After a while, Gully closed his eyes, and tears squeezed out.

"What do *you* want, then?" she asked softly.

His reply, when it came after a long pause, was so quiet that it was almost lost in the wind. "I just want my brother."

Emmaline knew that she couldn't cry, although she wanted to. One of them had to hold it together.

"It's okay," she said. "It's okay, Gully. We don't have to go in. We can go to my house if you want."

"I don't want to be near the machine," he said.

"I haven't had a chance to tell you. I've convinced my father to turn it off. I'm not even sure it still works, since it's the first time we've unplugged it. It's covered up with old blankets now."

He looked at her and rubbed his tears with the red scarf. "Really?" His thoughtful expression returned. "But that means you won't be able to see your mother's ghost anymore."

"I don't need to." Emmaline shook her head. "The time I had with her makes me who I am. So she's alive as long as I'm alive. You told me that."

He almost smiled then. "Do you think I was right about that?"

"You're always right," Emmaline said.

"Maybe not *always*."

"When it's important, you are."

That time, he did smile. He hadn't even planned to, but Emmaline brought it out of him. "I'd like to go inside," he said.

After they'd ordered their drinks, it was quiet for a long time. But the silence was comfortable. Gully had a lot to think about, and so did Emmaline.

Their cups were nearly empty when Gully spoke. "When you went missing, I thought

something happened to you," he said. "I can't lose you, too."

A ray of afternoon sun lit up Emmaline's eyes, making them bright and brilliant. "You'll never lose me," she said.

There was fear in his expression. "Nobody can make that promise."

"I can." She raised her chin. "You know everything about everything, but I know this."

She reached for the skeleton key tucked under her shirt. She unclasped its chain and stood to fit it around Gully's neck.

Gully curled his fingers around it. "You want to give me your mother's necklace?"

"I'm letting you borrow it, for as long as you need," she said. "My mother told me that when her house got demolished, it felt like watching a castle falling down. She didn't think the world would ever feel right again. But then time passed, and she went to school in a new city, and she got a new house, and she met my father and had me." It was magic, Emmaline thought, how many memories a single tiny key could hold.

Gully held the key up in his palm. It was smooth and brass, almost glowing in the afternoon sun.

"Maybe all of life is like that," he said. "Buildings getting demolished, and people finding new places to live."

Emmaline sat across from him again. It was strange, Gully without Oliver. She suspected it would be a long time before she stopped waiting for Oliver to come running through the door. It was very much like carrying a key to a door that no longer existed.

She held her hand out across the table, and Gully took it without hesitation. There was plenty that she wanted to say to him, but when thoughts were big, words felt too small.

Her father had been right, she realized. Even without saying a word, she and Gully knew what they meant to each other. They always had.

After their cups had been emptied, Emmaline said, "There's something I want to show you."

Emmaline led them to the door, and for once, Gully was the one who followed.

After the warmth of the café, the air felt that much colder. Gully unwound one of his scarves—the green one—and draped it over Emmaline's shoulders.

She smiled. "Thank you."

They walked the rest of the way in silence, Gully counting the seconds between cracks in the sidewalk. He didn't ask where Emmaline was taking them; he didn't seem to care. A world without Oliver in it was aimless; there were just steps and buildings and thoughts that flew up and up and up until they disappeared in the sky.

But when the church came into view, Gully tensed. He stopped walking.

The tower clock was just beginning the first of its chimes to mark the hour.

Emmaline stopped walking, too. "It's okay," she said. "We aren't going to go in there."

They often passed the church on their way to the park, or to the small theater that charged half price for sweets on the third Sunday of each month. Gully had always admired it. The tall arched windows, the bright glass, the clock chimes that were loud and angry and cheerful all at the same time. But now when he looked at the wide stone steps, he saw his brother's casket being carried up by pallbearers, and his mother going weak at the knees on the way in, and again on the way out.

Emmaline looped her arm around his. "This way," she said, and began leading him across the street. They used the crosswalk, but Gully didn't count the spaces between the white painted lines. He counted the bell chimes.

Across the street from the church, there was a bank. It was closed, the lights off and the blinds drawn over the windows. Emmaline began walking down the alleyway beside the bank.

"Where are we going?" Gully asked.

She looked over her shoulder, and her eyes were bright and playful. "It's better if I show you. Come on."

There was a fire escape on the side of the bank, and Emmaline climbed on top of a stack of wooden crates to pull down the ladder.

"Be careful," Gully said.

"It's safe," Emmaline promised, and held out a hand to help him up.

This was the sort of mischief Oliver would have loved—scaling a fire escape—and maybe that's why Gully went along with it.

The wind was sharper at the top of the bank, and the air was much colder.

Gully dug his hands into his coat pockets for warmth. "Emmy," he finally said, "what are we doing up here?"

She led him to the edge of the roof. From here, they had a perfect view of the church across the street. It didn't frighten Gully as

much from where he stood now. It seemed smaller. Less menacing.

"My father has been reading the paper a lot more these days, before he goes to work," Emmaline said. "He leaves it on the table, and sometimes I read it, too. That's how I heard."

"Heard what?" Gully asked.

Emmaline nudged him with her shoulder. "Just wait."

Despite the chill in the air, the sun was shining. Light glinted off the face of the church clock and the patches of ice on the sidewalks.

It was several minutes before the heavy oak doors of the church opened, and then the quiet afternoon was filled with the sound of laughter and cheers.

A bride and groom emerged, followed by a crowd of colorful dresses and matching brown suits.

"A wedding?" Gully said.

"Yes." Emmaline leaned her arms forward

against the ledge that framed the roof. She nodded to the woman in the white gown that puddled at her feet, rippling like water as she walked. "That's Granville's granddaughter."

"Granville," Gully echoed. "The ghost of your neighbors' brother."

Emmaline nodded, smiling. "I suppose she's inherited the money Granville was hiding. So, something good did come from that machine. Not what my father intended, maybe, but still. It's something."

"It's something," Gully echoed. His brows knit in thought. "I know that Oliver was right when he said it could be used to help people. I've always known that. But—"

Gully hesitated, and Emmaline inched closer, until her shoulder was pressed against his. "I know," she said. "It's for the best that it stay unplugged."

Together they watched the wedding procession disperse. Granville's granddaughter and her new husband climbed into the backseat of a sleek black limousine. The engine growled to life, and then they were on their way to start their lives together.

Emmaline rested her cheeks to her fists. "I hope they'll be happy," she said.

Gully rested his head on her shoulder, and she looped her arm around him. There was a time, not very long ago, when they both would have been startled by this sort of closeness, but now it was not only practical—it was important. Everything drifted out of reach one day. Everything could be taken away in a heartbeat. And if someone was still close enough to hold on to, then you should hold on.

Together, they watched the limousine drive farther down the road, until it was out of sight.

EPILOGUE

In the years that followed, Emmaline's house would become filled with many sounds. But the humming of the ghost machine was not one of them. There was the ticking of clocks, and the phone ringing, and eventually, though it took a while, lots and lots of laughter.

There were long conversations, the whistling of teakettles.

Emmaline's father lived to be very old. He saw Emmaline grow up, and attend college, and become an illustrator for children. He walked her down the aisle at her wedding, and he held each of his grandchildren right after they were born.

The house was filled with the giggling of children again when Emmaline brought them to visit, and new life, because life always got bigger and bigger with time. There were new things to cry about, and new things to laugh about, and new games to learn, and new songs to sing.

The ghost machine stayed in the basement, covered up by blankets, surrounded by boxes of decorations and old toys and clothes. When the children asked about the strange shape in the shadows, Emmaline would say, "Oh, that old thing? It's haunted. Best to leave it alone."

When her father was very old and he knew that it was his time, he gave Emmaline the house and everything inside of it. He told her that whatever she did with the machine now was up to her. He said, "You don't need to worry about me, Emmy. I'll be with your mother."

Often, Emmaline wondered if the machine still worked. In those years she said more goodbyes, some much harder than others. Gully wondered, too, and sometimes they talked about it, but there was always life to focus on, something happy to draw them back into the world of the living.

When Emmaline and Gully were very old, and the house was filled with moving boxes, they talked about it again. The house had become too big and too dusty. It was time for a new family to live there and fill it with their own lives. But there was still the matter of what to do with the machine.

"It seems a shame to destroy it," Gully said.

"It's been so long, I don't even know if it works," Emmaline said.

"We could try it."

"Really? Are you sure that's what you want?"

"I could never be sure, when it came to that thing. But then I suppose that's the point."

They talked about it for hours. They talked about it for days. And not just with words, but with glances, and with silence, too.

Eventually, the last of the boxes were packed. All the pictures were put away. Their children were grown and living in their own houses, with children and grandchildren of their own, and there was nothing left to talk about. In the morning, the machine would be loaded onto a van and carted off to the dump. This would be for the best—on that they had agreed.

"I say let's," Gully said. "Just once, before it's gone forever."

Emmaline smiled. "I was hoping you would say that."

They knew exactly which box to open with the scissors. They knew exactly which thing they'd feed the machine. They'd never had to say a word about it. They were each holding an end of Oliver's red scarf as they descended the basement steps.

They moved slowly. Their bones were tired, and they couldn't run the way they once had. But they weren't in any hurry.

Gully pulled the blankets from the machine, while Emmaline was the one to plug it back into the wall.

The machine's purple light flickered like a dying bulb, and then gradually gave off steadier, brighter rays.

For a long while, Emmaline and Gully stood together, watching the thing.

"It's been so long," Gully finally said. "Do you think he'd recognize me?"

Emmaline rested her head on his shoulder. "Of course," she answered. "I see him sometimes when I look at you."

"Even now?"

"Even now."

They looked at the scarf in their hands.

"We don't have to, if you're having second thoughts," Emmaline said.

Gully took a deep breath. Over a lifetime, he

had learned to speak about Oliver often, making him a part of their daily lives, the way he'd speak about the weather or what he'd had for breakfast. He'd told their children about him. He kept pictures in frames. But the thought of the boy he'd lost hurt him. Still. Always.

"One last hello," he said. "I'm ready for one last hello."

They held the red scarf up to the mouth of the machine. They let go at the same time, and it fluttered and swirled and disappeared as it fell.

Nothing happened.

And then, the machine started to rattle.

Acknowledgments

As ever, thank you to my family for their overwhelming support and love. Especially my little cousins, who are always asking me what I'm working on next.

Thank you to the greatest humans I have ever met: Beth Revis, Aprilynne Pike, Laini Taylor, Randi Oomens, Sabaa Tahir, all of whom always come up with something encouraging and clever to say during the times I've thought I was beyond encouragement. Thank you to my readers, for listening to my stories.

Thank you to my agent, Barbara Poelle; I ran out of clever ways to say thank you several years ago, and yet she still sticks by me. Thank you to the amazing team at Bloomsbury, from my editor, Cat Onder, to marketing and publicity, to the art department. Thank you to Marcos Calo, who created a cover more beautiful and true to Emmaline's story than I could have imagined. Words will never be able to convey my gratitude.